CARAVANSERAI

THE CHRONICLES OF ALCINIA BOOK VII

MIRIAM NEWMAN

❀ Created with Vellum

CHAPTER 1

Jadda was dying.

The slow drip of water echoed the beat of her grandmother's heart. Windows of their second story apartment above Someno's caravanserai funneled a bit of merciful coolness, but it was summer, when water grew scarce and the sun strong. Tenderly, Serafina sponged her Jadda's wizened face, attempting to impart what comfort she could.

"Peace, peace," she murmured. With long strokes, she soothed Jadda Marouka's deeply lined cheeks. Her grandmother had reached five tens of years, a good life span for the Domidian poor. Now, her umber eyes sunk into a nest of wrinkles followed the motion of Serafina's hand, but she could no longer speak. She had been that way for some time, ceaselessly attended by Serafina and her mother. But they could only hold back death just so long.

"All our words are said," Serafina told her gently.

The instructive lives of thousands drifted through the caravanserai where travelers came. Listening to them had made her, in some ways, older than her five-and-ten years.

"Sharp as a sword's point," her mother always said of her, with a smile. At such times, Serafina knew Ummi was thinking of the man who had fathered her. He had been one of countless thousands of Omanis and Havacians who conquered her country... a foreigner...a camel rider...a man well acquainted with the use of a sword. Yet to her mother, he seemed to have been the focal point of her life—the thing after which nothing else mattered quite so much.

Once, they had lived in a square house on the marketplace where Ummi sold melons. Then, her mother had become able to afford a desirable spot in the caravanserai and a stall for varied wares, and their lives had improved. Their spacious quarters above the bazaar were more than adequately furnished. Her grandmother rested on fine-woven blankets and they were never short of food. Her mother's shop on the lower level was a place where weary travelers could purchase virtually anything their journeys required. Much of this was paid for by the father she had never seen, so she knew he was aware that she existed. His payments arrived as regularly as the wax and wane of the moon, delivered by an Omani paymaster's clerk. What camel rider had such funds?

No one would tell her, and now any chance of learning more had vanished along with her grandmother's speech. She would never know whose face she bore, because Ummi and cousin Imrun said she looked like him.

Already tall and broad-shouldered, with a face more striking than pretty, she was becoming a woman. She had to cover herself carefully now, because men were becoming interested. Wildly waving hair from her unknown father, black as midnight, attracted them. Her curiously greenish eyes, so different than dark Domidian eyes, drew attention, and her skin was lighter than most because of her Havacian blood. It was unseemly for a girl to receive so much notice, and soon Cousin Imrun would select a husband for her. Since her grandfather's death, he had assumed his place as head of the family, other men having perished in the Great War, and she knew whom Imrun had in mind for her.

Jalal, the young clerk he had taken in from one of the last internment camps to work for him, was nice enough. Secretly, though, she had always suspected Imrun took Jalal not out of charity, but because he envisioned a marriage between them. It was her mother's money he was after, though not directly, because he feared the Omanis would arrest him if he took it. Instead, he would get it through Jalal's involvement in her business, which Jalal would take one day on Serafina's behalf. She would never see a single coin. They would take everything when her mother died and she would be like every other woman she knew except her mother—dependent on a husband, fortunate if he was kind, miserable if he was not, but in any case never free.

If she succeeded in refusing Jalal, which was unlikely, then the alternative would no doubt be a rich old man smelling of garlic and the hookah, who nonetheless would father many children on her, then die when she had passed her years of attractiveness. The law prescribed only that she be left enough money to support her and keep her in her home for a year. One year. Then, if she had not remarried, she would be at the mercy of his sons while they took everything he had owned, which would include everything she brought to the marriage.

They thought she didn't know. They took her for a stupid girl.

Behind her, she heard the soft sound of her mother's sandals on the steps to the apartment, coming from the stall below. Now in her third decade, Pescia was still a beautiful woman, raven-haired, with flashing dark eyes and a graceful smile.

"Do you need me below?" Serafina asked.

But Pescia shook her head. "No, Imrun is at the stall."

Her cousin was there, watching to see that nothing was filched, bargaining with customers for the saddle blankets, girths and straps, tents, rugs and blankets, even live chickens they needed for their trek into the desert. Theirs was an urban caravanserai, sprawling beyond the walls of Someno, a port city. All goods came through the caravanserai, where they were taxed: dates and spices, woven rugs and camel hair fabric from Domidia's desert...wine and oil, timber and fish sauce on ships from Omana. The former enemies did good trade with each other, if nothing else.

"How is she?" Pescia inquired, reaching the top of the steps. The staircase ended directly in front of their apartment. Others had to turn and walk the narrow walkway of boards that wound around the second level of the caravanserai like a vine. The arrangement gave them ready access, but every neighbor passed their door on the way to their own. It was a very communal and rarely quiet way to live.

"The same," Serafina said, but she knew she lied. Hourly, she could see the light fading from Jadda's eyes.

Pescia came to her mother's bedside, looking down at her with a smile. "Rest, my Ummi," she said softly, as though not wishing to disturb the older woman's hard-earned slumber. Soon, it would be eternal sleep. Then she and Serafina would wash the body of the woman who had been their staunch pillar and wind her in five lengths of the finest linen the caravanserai had to offer. After that, any who wished to come could pray over Jadda until priests arrived to ritually bind her body with four ceremonial ropes, one at the head, two in the middle, one at the feet.

Mourners following to the grave might number in the scores. Though she had no family left aside from Pescia and

Serafina, Jadda had made many friends among the folk of the caravanserai. Bound in everyday life, even unto death, they buried their own. Jadda would have a simple grave in the sandy soil of Someno, there being no time to return her to her native village of Amrah, where her husband lay. That village had been obliterated in the war, never to rise again. It was only a graveyard now. Nobody went there anymore.

And so they would mark her resting place in Someno with a wreath, where tangled winds from desert and sea would eventually destroy it, leaving her alone and unknown except by family. Once they were gone, so was she.

Serafina looked with pity on the face of her grandmother, who had achieved no more in life. Neither would she, unless she fought for it.

Reassured that her mother still lived, Pescia turned wordlessly, going back down the steps to be sure Imrun was not pocketing part of their gains. It would in all likelihood be Serafina who saw her grandmother from life, but she did not resent it. Jadda had always been good to her, not holding it against her that she was the daughter of a heathen who worshipped a Northern Goddess. It was rare these days, anyway, to see a Havacian, though there were still many Omanis in their country, ruling it.

"Peace," Serafina whispered once again, though her heart was rebellious. It was true that she did not hunger or thirst, which was a blessing. But she did not know who she was.

"Who was he?" she murmured, expecting no answer. It was only a forlorn question to herself, so it was all the more shocking when a reply came in a choked, dry whisper.

"Em-perator," Jadda barely breathed.

Where had her grandmother's mind gone? They called him Father of Omana, yes. But the man who had taken that Seat some years before, cousin of the Havacian King who brought Domidia to its knees, was no friend of theirs.

"I will bring you drink," Serafina offered, though she was no longer sure Jadda could swallow even the cold tea they sometimes gave her. A creature of the desert winds, she was returning to them. She would die for lack of drink through sheer inability to swallow it.

She tried, sputtering and gasping with even the slowest, most careful feeding of liquid through her parched lips. At last, Serafina had no more heart to urge it on her and eased her head gently back on her pillow. Jadda gave her the ghost of a smile.

"Knows," her grandmother said, and then closed her eyes. Serafina felt one last grasp of her fingers on her young, strong hand. All of Jadda's life had been hard except for the last part, eased by the money Serafina's father sent. For that, Serafina supposed she had to be grateful. But a sense of abandonment and fear swept over her, as real and pressing as the knowledge of her grandmother's death.

Sliding her fingers up Jadda's bony wrist, she felt in vain for the beat of life.

Silently, she bent for a moment over the poor tortured body on the bed. "Go into the Garden," she whispered. All the deserving went to the Garden of the One God, there to be reunited with loved ones. Jadda was walking in peace now, free until the Rising at the Last, when all souls would be met.

* * *

MAROUKA, Serafina's treasured Jadda, was buried with much courtesy. At dawn of the next day, mourners began to arrive, their soft voices blending with the sounds of creaking wagon wheels, plaintive complaints of camels and the bleating of goats. They were the reassuring sounds of morning that were all Serafina could ever remember hearing. But her grandmother would never hear them again.

From her place next to Jadda's bier, where she sat cross-legged on a mat, Serafina watched people arrive. Some bore ceremonial foods, some small gifts, others only themselves. Her mother greeted all of them, standing at the door while Serafina remained respectfully in the place of mourning.

"What a good grand daughter you are," her mother's friend Saleema greeted her, looking down where she sat on the floor. "Your Jadda was always so proud of you."

Serafina bowed her head modestly. She was dressed that day in the head-to-toe white of mourning, with a mask over the lower part of her face. It would conceal signs of grief and also shield her from the inevitable blowing sand that accompanied every interment, disturbed by gravediggers. Ummi had already paid them and also paid for professional mourners, since Imrun was too cheap to do it. Marouka had been Pescia's mother, not his, he said rudely, and so Pescia paid. She always paid. Why she should follow his orders when she was the one who received money, Serafina was not sure. But that was how it was in Domidia.

"You are kind, my mother's friend," she said, much more formal than she usually was with Saleema, whom she had known all her life. But it was a day of formalities.

"I have brought bakoosh," the older woman said, indicating the wicker basket she bore, full of freshly baked round bread traditional at funerals. Its shape signified the circle of life ending at the grave and would be served at the funeral feast along with ground chickpeas, dates, green onions, cheeses and curds, a seethed kid one merchant had donated, a mound of marinated chicken from another, persimmons and pomegranates, ground sesame mixed with honey and cinnamon, and endless cups of coffee and tea. Everything was contributed by those who attended. Pescia had been busy but not, at least, with feeding people. Instead, it was her day to be fed and comforted by her friends.

A seemingly endless stream greeted Serafina once they had spoken to her mother, all of them surreptitiously studying the shrouded figure on its rope bed. She and Pescia had attended to the wrapping meticulously, knowing it would be judged. It was perfect.

There was a slight stir at the door, where she saw Imrun, Jalal and Imrun's wife, Hestar. Her cousin's clerk, tall and slender with youth, was attired in white robes circled by the black sash of mourning. He was a little older than Serafina and a newly-sprung jet beard stood out below his impeccably wound turban. Serafina smiled beneath her mask. Jalal was inordinately proud of the facial hair that marked him as a man.

That realization erased her smile. The thought brought an intimation of danger that warred with her customary fondness for him. The time for childish games had passed. Now, she feared there were other games Jalal wished to play, while she did not.

From across the room, where Imrun spoke quietly to Pescia, his eyes met hers. They were the usual dark eyes of Domidia, so different from her own, and today they were somber. Imrun and Hestar made no attempt to restrain him as he crossed the room to speak with her. It was a time of mourning and they were in public, so much would be permitted that was otherwise frowned upon. Pursuit of one's future wife was conducted discreetly unless she continued to refuse, in which case the groom and his friends might abduct her. Even the bride knew it would happen, so it was only token resistance. If she made trouble after that, she would be beaten. But most girls accepted their lot, becoming dutiful wives and mothers.

"The good God comfort you," he said, reaching her. "May He bring you peace."

The ritual words said and acknowledged by her nod, Jalal dropped his formal tone. "I know what she meant to you."

"Yes," Serafina acknowledged. For the first time, she felt intensely awkward in his presence. She could not be accused of being alone with him, the room was filled with people, yet he was paying her marked attention. It was as if he was conveying that they enjoyed a certain amount of intimacy, and she did not want that from him or want others to see it between them. It was only a short distance from people's expectations to the accomplishment of their goals.

Fortunately, just then there was a larger disturbance in the doorway as the guests made way immediately for two priests who entered with ceremonial ties.

"They have come for her," Jalal said, and offered his hand for Serafina to rise. Her duty now done, she must make way for them. She put her hand obediently in his, feeling his strength as he helped her to her feet, and stood beside him, silent as the priests gently and efficiently roped the pitifully small figure on the bed.

"Sshh," he said quietly, and she realized he had seen the start of tears in her eyes. His expression was kind and he did not release her hand. Behind her, she heard her mother and relatives moving into place while everyone in the room stepped back, silent and respectful.

"The Lord is merciful." The two priests chanted in counterpoint, the better for their prayers to reach Heaven, while helpers transferred the body to an ornate carrying board garlanded with flowers, where a forehead band and one at her ankles secured the deceased so they could get her down the staircase. They did this frequently. Many people in the caravanserai died—of old age, illness or accident. It was a place intense in both life and death and Serafina had absorbed it like a sponge, so she just watched, silent as men bore the body of her grandmother down the steps she had trodden so many times until she could not do it anymore.

And now she was dead, her burdens eased. Serafina knew she should be happy for Jadda, but she could not. Despite her misgivings, it was a comfort to have Jalal's strong presence at her side. Perhaps she could accustom herself to it, she thought, even knowing as she did it that she lied.

CHAPTER 2

The hired mourners earned their money, wailing pitifully as the solemn gathering moved through the streets, where customary noises ceased. Those who had known Marouka followed her, so it was only strangers who fell silent and cast their eyes down, clearing the path of their children and flocks for the procession to pass.

Serafina kept her eyes down, as well, still feeling her hand in Jalal's. He had not let go, guiding her carefully over uneven stones that might trip her while she wore unaccustomed, dressy sandals much nicer than her usual footwear.

"Are you all right?" he asked quietly, and she just nodded. She had neither eaten nor drunk, as all the bounty brought for mourners would remain untouched until they returned from the funeral. The sun was mounting the sky, so his concern was well-founded, but Serafina was stronger than she looked. Her willowy figure was uncommon among Domidians, but it did not denote weakness.

That was why she neither flinched nor faltered at the grave, not even when the priests' helpers handed her the customary blue-green urn containing three handfuls of soil removed from Jadda's grave. Every grain would be returned to the earth that had provided it, along with the bones of the deceased. From dust all came and to dust they were returned.

"Do not weep, Daughter," her mother murmured when it came Serafina's turn to empty her urn. Below her, she could see her grandmother's shrouded form, tiny and lonely in her final resting place. Dry-eyed, she upended the colored urn she would keep as a memento of Jadda's life.

The insignificance and futility of it struck her like a blow. Of her grandmother, she would have memories, some expensive jewelry that could be worn only in private for her husband, and a blue-green urn. That was all.

"You will look beautiful in her jewels one day," Jalal said softly, an attempted consolation, but it chilled her. Brides wore such jewels on the night of their wedding—a jeweled choker, bracelets and anklets. Most girls were thrilled by the prospect that denoted their entrance into womanhood, but Serafina was repulsed. Hunting dogs also wore collars and shackles. It was not Jalal's fault that this sprang from Imrun's urging, but with a sudden flash of rage, she knew she would never be so imprisoned, no matter what she had to do. She would not die as Jadda had done. There had to be more to life.

* * *

THE MOURNERS HAD GONE as the sun set late. Summer hours were long, and hot, and Serafina and her mother moved only slowly around the apartment, tidying up. Pescia's friends had left them little to do. Jadda's empty bed was freshly changed and neatly made and now Ummi drew her few possessions from a bedside table.

Serafina had abandoned her mask, so her mother could

see her wary expression as she handed over Jadda's prized silk pouch closed with a jeweled tassel.

"These are yours now," Pescia said.

Serafina had never seen them; she had only known they were there. Most little girls would have tried to peek, but even when she was young she had known what they represented and ignored them. Gingerly, she opened the pouch, reaching inside, feeling a fine filigreed gold choker. Pulling it out, she saw it was ringed with close-set rectangular diamonds that formed a band for the throat. Two bracelets were identically crafted, and two anklets, and there were long earrings with gold hooks and wire decorated with glittering diamond chips. The jewels were worth a small fortune —the only thing aside from her clothes that Jadda had owned. No woman ever had more unless, like Pescia, she had entered a trade, or unless she sold her body.

She glanced up at her mother, not wanting to seem ungrateful, yet bursting with questions her grandmother's death had stirred up anew.

"Thank you, Ummi."

"They are yours now," Pescia repeated. "I will not marry, so they come to you."

Despite her good looks, her mother had never taken up with another man and Serafina wondered if she was not sometimes lonely.

"Could you not?" she questioned.

Her mother shrugged. "Why should I? I have what I need. A husband would only take all that I own while never having worked for it."

"But you would have me do so."

Her mother looked uncomfortable, but resolute.

"I cannot leave you my business," she said. "It can go only to a man. The only way I can ensure your support is to find a husband who will continue it and provide for you."

"And Jalal would be your choice?" Serafina pressed.

"It would be a good match," Pescia reasoned. "He is fond of you and I think he would be a kind husband."

Serafina had seldom argued with her mother, but she sensed the noose tightening around her. "I cannot help my feelings or the lack of them. Besides..."

"Besides what?" her mother prompted.

"Besides, Jalal feels what I do not. I can see it when he looks at me. Today he told me I would be beautiful in Jadda's jewels. You know what that means."

"That means he is looking at you as a wife," her mother said. "There is no reason he should not. A man has a right to view his wife in that way."

"But you did not marry!"

"I did not marry because Imrun sold me to a passing soldier who left me with child. No man would marry such a woman."

Serafina repressed sudden tears. "I was a shame to you."

"No shame," Pescia insisted. "I wanted you very much. It was war, Serafina. Many women were left in the same way."

"Then my father raped you."

Her mother gasped. "He did not! Your father kept me safe from those men, and when his army sent him elsewhere, he gave me money to begin my melon stand so that I need not sleep with other men for my living. I did not want another after him."

It was the most her mother had ever said to her of her conception. Serafina did not even know her father's name.

"But he must have known about me. He sent more money."

Pescia nodded ever so slightly. "Yes, he knew. The Army sent him here once more, during the rebellion. He saw you then."

"He saw me? What did he say?"

Pescia smiled, tight and bitter. "He said he was married and had a son, but that he was sorry and would send money."

"He was sorry I was born?"

"No, he wanted you to have whatever you needed."

"That is a lot of money," Serafina said thoughtfully. "How would a soldier have that much?"

"He was an officer," Pescia explained. "Not a common soldier. I think his family had money. He spent quite freely."

Serafina knew some officers of good family still commanded a Domidian camel corps, but they were Omanis.

"I thought he was Havacian."

"And part Omani," Pescia said. "Many of them went north after Omana fell. I think he said his grandfather was one of them. He spoke it, anyway. Looked it, too."

"And I look like him?"

Her mother's expression softened. "You do. So much. He was very handsome, I thought."

"So you wanted to be with him, then?"

"Oh, child." Her mother took her hand, sinking down on Jadda's bed, drawing Serafina with her. "We were desperate after the war and Imrun saved us the only way he could. But your father was good to me."

"Did you love him?"

Her mother looked down. "Yes. But he never returned."

"Well, I do not love Jalal," Serafina said, softly but defiantly. "I tell you, Ummi, I will not marry him. And if he forces it, I will make his life a living hell."

"My God, what have I brought into the world?"

Serafina rose without her mother's consent, leaving her jeweled pouch on Jadda's bed.

"A soldier's daughter."

* * *

THEY SPOKE no more of it, Serafina returned the jewels to her grandmother's bedside table, and life went on as before. Yet mother and daughter were conscious of a new space opened between them.

"I do not know what to do with her, Saleema," Pescia confessed to her friend, sitting at tea. "She is adamant that she will not accept Jalal and I dare not repeat it to Imrun. They will only steal her from me."

"Serafina is a good girl," Saleema pointed out, "but you know her stubbornness. If she says she will not accept Jalal, then she is unlikely to do it willingly and perhaps not even unwillingly. And a bitter, contentious wife is no gift to anyone. The boy does not deserve that."

"I know," Pescia moaned.

"Go to the Omanis," her friend suggested. "Whoever sends that money, he is a man of some standing. They may protect you."

Pescia just shook her head. "They cannot protect me from my stall burning down during the night and, honestly, I do not think they care. They bring me money, but only to throw it at my feet."

"Yes, they are still enemies." Her friend sighed. "I do not think we will ever be rid of them."

"No," Pescia agreed. "They are too afraid we will invade them again, as if we could do it now."

"You will have to let Jalal and his friends take her and hope it turns out well," Saleema counseled.

Pescia stared into the distance. "That will not be enough."

The other woman shrugged. "It will have to be. I love her like a little niece, but you have to admit the girl is willful. Jalal will have his hands full with her. Perhaps having a child will settle her spirit."

"She is still too much a child herself," Pescia lamented.

"She pesters me unceasingly to know who her father is. She even plagued my mother about it on her deathbed."

Saleema clucked her disapproval. "Well, you know who he is, do you not?"

"Of course I know."

"Then tell her."

"I *have* told her." Pescia could not keep the exasperation from her voice. "She will not be satisfied. Jalal can accept being an orphan, but Serafina cannot even accept what I tell her. He is much more mature. She does not realize how lucky she is."

Saleema sighed in sympathy. "Let them take her, then. He will not hurt her."

Pescia just gave her friend a long, enigmatic look. "I lived through the war. You were too young to remember. Men do evil things. All those men who slaughtered us—they had wives and sisters and daughters, I'm sure. Yet what they did to our women was unspeakable."

"We are not at war," Saleema pointed out.

Pescia laughed shortly. "We will be, if they take her."

CHAPTER 3

The days were growing shorter. Date palms had been harvested and olive trees had also given up their fruits. Serafina sensed that her time was growing shorter, too, and anxiety haunted her days and, particularly, her nights.

Rain showers began to blow in from the ocean, fewer fishing boats went out, and now the time to harvest the flocks had come. She always felt sorry watching them come into the caravanserai. These were the ones not to be bred nor fed through the winter. Ummi knew the fate of the animals distressed her and was much more lenient with her then, so that Serafina began spending some hours when she was not needed away from the apartment, going to the shoreline where it was cooler.

Now, however, she found that she was looking behind her even there, sensing that Imrun might be running out of patience as her six-and-ten birthday approached. But Serafina had an answer for that. Weeping but determined, she hacked off her hair. There would be much about which to weep in the days ahead. The loss of her hair was only the beginning.

She was taller than most Domidian women, and rangier. From a secret stash in Jada's beside table, which she knew her mother no longer touched because it grieved her, she took out clothing readily available from the bazaar—men's robes that concealed her few womanly charms, heavier sandals than women wore, and a turban she wound inexpertly, but well enough for its flap to conceal most of her face. Even if she did not draw it, her lack of a beard would be excused by age, and her angular jaw and aquiline nose might well belong to a boy.

Giddy with newfound freedom, she escaped the confines of the apartment and the caravanserai at every opportunity, cunning as any animal trying to escape its cage. Her heart was burdened, knowing that the cozy apartment and busy market that had always been her safety and comfort now served to entrap her. But they would, and she knew it, and she would have none of it.

DRESSED AS A BOY, she went outside the confines of the caravanserai to one of the private markets on the other side of Someno. Many of those bought damaged wares from the caravanserai and sold them at reduced prices to the poor and Serafina had seldom been there, but she knew where they were.

It was after mid-day, a time when the remaining heat beginning to ebb from Domidia still rendered many inhabitants slow and sleepy. Hoping to find one like that, she turned into a small corner shop that looked seedy and rundown. She would not get as good a price there, but neither did proprietors of such establishments ask many questions.

Wending her way through hanging baskets hitting her in the head, she secured her face covering one more time, reaching beneath her robes to the precious packet secreted inside. A gap-toothed man nearly as old as Jadda lounged behind his counter, sharp-eyed for those who would pilfer his goods, but otherwise not much concerned with someone he judged to be an adolescent boy. One boy alone was not much of a threat, though a group of them could be pick-pockets.

"Do you seek sale or pawn?" the merchant inquired.

"Sale," Serafina replied, lowering her voice. "My mother will have no further need of these."

The man's eyes narrowed as she drew out Jadda's jewels.

Serafina made a gesture of mourning.

"She has gone to the Garden," she explained, telling herself it was not exactly a lie. It was where her grandmother had gone, after all. "There is no one left to need these and I can better use the money for them."

"May the Gods give you peace," the merchant said, by rote, without emotion. Instead, his eyes were trained on Jadda's jewels, which were now hers. But not for long. It was a wrench, so deep and soul-searing that she would not be able to keep to her plans if she let herself think about it, so she didn't. Her palms were sweaty and her heart beat like a drum, but she let the merchant lift them from her hand, appraising them.

"Old-fashioned," he said. "Still, the jewels may be worked into something better. Thirty and four dinars for the lot."

The look she gave this shopkeeper suggested that a dagger in his gullet would have suited her perfectly well. She had perfected that flinty-eyed look by haggling with customers in her mother's stall.

"Thirty and six," he amended.

Serafina took them from his hand. "I would do better to trade for camels."

Actually, that was true, except what would she do with camels? If her plan succeeded, she would be riding someone else's.

"Thirty and eight," he said, "and that is all."

She let him hang for a moment, then nodded. Something inside of her shuddered, but it was done. He pocketed them quickly, her inheritance disappearing inside the deep pocket of a robe that was none too clean, but from the other pocket he counted out her money. She knew she was fortunate. He could have kept the jewels and beaten her senseless with the club she glimpsed behind his counter, preying on her youth, claiming that she had tried to rob him. Perhaps Jadda had given her luck despite her betrayal.

Saying nothing, she turned and picked her way out through aisles crowded with junk and into the teeming streets, tears filming her eyes.

That was why she never saw him. Abruptly, a shape loomed up in front of her—one that did not move. She ran nose first into a chest she knew, stopping with a telltale gasp.

"What are you doing?" Jalal asked.

She looked up at him. He smiled—cynically.

"You cannot hide those green eyes," he said. "What foolishness is this? You wear robes in the public market. Gods, girl, you will be flogged."

It was a distinct possibility, especially if he made a scene. Instead, he grabbed her arm as if disciplining a little brother, turning her in the direction of the harbor.

"I ask you again," he said, low but threatening. "What are you doing?"

"Selling my grandmother's jewels."

"Yes, I could see that." She realized then that it was Jalal, not Imrun, that she had sensed following her. "Why?"

"I have need of money."

"For what?" He sounded torn between laughter and astonishment at her bravado.

"For freedom," she hissed.

She saw him glance about quickly to see if they were attracting attention. They weren't, and he pulled her into an alleyway between shops selling chickens and tobacco. The acrid smells of chicken shit and smoke assaulted her senses.

"What in the name of the Great God are you talking about?" he demanded.

She wrenched her arm free, grateful when he released it.

"I know what Imrun plans," she said, breathlessly. "I will not have it."

His expression clouded. "You will not have me, you mean."

"I will not have any man," she said. "Not yet. There are things I must do first."

"What things?"

"I need freedom first," she said, nearly pleading with him. "It is not you, Jalal. But I am not ready to be anyone's wife, much less a mother. It is too soon for me."

He was silent. She knew she had hurt him. But dishonesty would hurt even more, in the end.

"I do not even know who I am," she said. "I know my mother, but not my father. Jadda is dead. There is no one else but Imrun."

"There is me," he said quietly. "I do not know who my father was, either—nor my mother. They were just bodies in the street. I cannot even remember them. I like Imrun no better than you do."

"Yet you take orders from him," she pointed out. "Why?"

"Why?" He laughed, shortly. "For money, of course. A man must make a living somehow."

"Selling blankets?" she goaded him. "Still bearing his abuse when he is old and toothless, only because he has the money from Ummi's stall? What sort of life is that for a man? You are worth more than that."

He didn't answer.

"Don't you see?" she asked. "We are both trapped by his greed. Can you think I wish to leave my mother? Of course I don't! But if I don't, I will live under his thumb."

She looked up at him. "What would you do if you could do as you wished?"

"Raise horses," he said, to her astonishment. "Blood stock such as they race. But what would you do? What can a woman do?"

"Not much," she said, bitterly.

He nodded. "And that is why you dressed as a boy."

"It is safer," she replied nervously.

"You don't know how true that is." He looked down at her, somberly. Now that she thought about it, she had not seen Jalal smile or laugh much in a long time. He was unhappy. She was not the only one.

"You are a woman, Serafina," he said. "There are dangers in that you do not yet appreciate."

"Oh, I appreciate them," she said. "I know what could happen to me."

"Then let them happen with me," he said, quietly, raising her chin to meet his eyes. "I would never mistreat you."

She couldn't bear his gaze. "I know that. But...I can't, Jalal. Not yet. I have...a hunger...that I can't satisfy."

"That is why you need a husband," he said.

"For what?" She struggled to keep contempt from her voice. He did not deserve that. Life had given him few choices, after all. "Selling rugs and having a child every year until I am used up and you have no more money from supporting them?"

He sighed, reaching for her hand. Nervously, she let him take it. He was bigger and stronger than she was. If he wanted to take her by force, he could do it.

But he didn't try. Gently, he kneaded her palm.

"And what would you do if you could do what you wanted?" He turned her question back on her.

"Find my father."

"What?"

"It took me a long time to understand what Jadda was trying to tell me. I asked her...again...just before she died. She said, "Emperator." I thought she was dreaming. But then she said, "Knows."

Jalal was looking at her blankly.

"Don't you see? My father, whoever he is, has money. He has been sending it for years. He is not a common soldier. He is somebody the Emperator knows. Ummi said he had a private tent and sent correspondence to the Havacian king. He was someone of importance, perhaps even a great deal. Imrun will tell me nothing, but Jadda was trying to say that the Emperator knows who he is."

Jalal hooted quietly, aware of the crowds passing their alley. "And so you will do what? Go to Omana and ask him?"

"Exactly. Our camel trains go up there. They are always looking for boys to tend the animals. I have money for the journey and I speak Omani." Most of the merchants did. They needed it for business. Jalal spoke it, too.

He was looking at her like she had grown two heads.

"I can't believe you."

"Well, I can't believe you," she shot back. "Staying here to be Imrun's lap dog."

That had wounded him. She could see it in his set expression. Now he would probably drag her back and marry her despite everything.

"Don't try to stop me," she begged. "If you don't want to go, that's fine, but I do."

"What are you saying?"

She stopped abruptly, aware for the first time that she had meant something. She hadn't meant to mean it, but there it was.

"Come with me," she said. "I have money. We would have to go now, before winter, but we could make it. And after that, they say Omana is a garden, with oranges and lemons everywhere, and rivers such as we have never seen. Hanging gardens. Baths with warm waters."

"Not for people like us," he objected. "Those things are for the rich."

"Well, what if my father is rich?" she persisted. "I think he is."

"And you will just knock on his door and say oh, hello, I'm Serafina, you left me in Domidia, tell your wife I have come? He will give you nothing but his boot in your rear. Omanis don't like us."

"No, but they do business with us," she pointed out. "And we both know business. Perhaps you might get to raise those horses. Who knows? But you'll never find out, staying here with Imrun."

"It would break Hesta's heart," he objected. "She at least has been kind to me."

"And it will break Ummi's heart," Serafina said bluntly. "Can you think I don't know it? But all her life, she fought for her freedom as well as she could. I can do nothing less."

For the first time, Jalal looked confused. Tempted? She wasn't sure. But he wasn't being adamant with her.

"Come on," she coaxed. "I'm hungry. Let's get some

kabobs and something to drink and talk about it. It's getting late."

"Yes," he agreed, looking at the sun.

"People will think I'm your brother," she said. "No one will know. And then maybe go to the camel yard and see if a train is forming."

"Oh, a train is always forming," Jalal noted, "especially going into winter."

Serafina knew that was true. It was why she had waited to carry out her plan. Camels that had made the long trek north and back again were rested over the summer months, then sent out again to the salt mines where they could pick up a cargo of slabs to be taken to Omana. From there, the precious commodity could be shipped to the rest of the world, which would pay dearly for it. Many young boys made their first trips north in the fall, beginning lives that they hoped would take them to the level of caravanners—men who led lines of camels through the trackless wastes they could read and others could not or feared to try. It was a dangerous life, but some became wealthy. If it was business he wanted, Jalal could find it there.

She looked up at him again, smiling with her eyes since he could see nothing else of her face. "What can it hurt?"

"Everything," he said, and she held her breath. Either he would go with her or drag her back, and there was nothing she could do to stop it either way.

"Please?"

It was unfair and she knew it. He was a man and he wanted her. She was using it against him. If he agreed, she could even be committing herself to what she had just said she didn't want, or something close to it. But hadn't her mother done the same thing?

Like mother, like daughter. A woman must use what weapons she had.

CHAPTER 4

Dressed in men's robes, hair shorn, breasts bound, Serafina suddenly experienced freedom such as she had never known, walking with Jalal. No one spared them a glance.

It was a different world from the one she had known and she was still suspicious that he was only humoring her, planning all the while to take her home. Yet Jalal seemed both relaxed and interested in a way he never was at the caravanserai, where he followed Imrun's instructions faithfully, but without enthusiasm. Here, he seemed more alive.

She realized that she would be unable to relate to him as she usually did if she wanted to pull off a disguise. A younger brother would be deferential, but not timid the way a woman would be. And so she spoke freely to him as they ate at a table at one of the outdoor markets, where the only customers were men and boys.

"Do you come here often?" she asked.

He nodded. "When I can."

She was puzzled. All they needed was at the caravanserai. Why would Jalal frequent such neighborhoods? They were not necessarily dangerous, but definitely a step down. The scent of unwashed bodies offended her nose, there were stray dogs and cats foraging for scraps, and few women. Those who did venture into the streets were accompanied by husbands and shopped busily. They did not lounge at tables eating kabobs and passing hookahs.

Fortunately, Jalal did not share that vice or any other that she knew of. He was clear-eyed and direct.

"I feel more at home here," he said. "It seems to me I came from such a place."

All she knew—all anyone knew—was that he had been found in a poor quarter of Amrah after Havacians and Omanis had burned it to the ground. Wandering in the street, he had been scooped up before mounted Havacians rampaging through the city could run over him and placed in one of the internment camps the victors set up. Horrible places. Even going with Imrun had been preferable and so he had come to Someno.

"You cannot remember?" she asked.

He shook his head. "Not really. It is just a sense."

It was something they had in common. He knew nothing of his parents and she knew precious little of her father.

"We are out of our minds, you know," he said, making her choke on the lamb she was eating.

"Are we?"

"Sane people don't run away from a safe life into the desert."

"Then who goes with the caravans?" she asked.

"Those with nothing better to do."

"Or those looking for something better," she rebutted.

"What do you know of camels?" Jalal was pursuing a different line of thought.

"Nothing," she admitted. "You can teach me."

"They are vicious," he said. "Will you start screaming like

a girl the first time you are bitten? Because you will be, I assure you."

"No." She licked her fingers. "I will start cursing like a man."

He gave her a grudging smile. "Perhaps you will, at that. Are you sure you can maintain the disguise?"

"Why not? I am told all the time I am not womanly. I am too tall, too plain, too bold, too outspoken. I make a poor woman, apparently."

"You never seemed that way to me," Jalal said. "I think you are beautiful."

Serafina promptly disclosed her gender by blushing. It was obvious with her lighter coloring and Jalal laughed. He had finished his meal.

"Are you ready to see the camels? I warn you, though, they stink."

"They can't be much worse than this," she said, gesturing to the crowd. Water was free from the public wells, but apparently most of them abstained.

"The stench of the poor," Jalal said, unconcerned. "If we go into the desert, we will be sharing it soon enough."

* * *

HE HAD LIED TO HER, of course. Not about his prospective plan, because he was sorely tempted to join her lunatic venture. No, he had lied about what he remembered.

Jalal had forgotten nothing. He remembered the smoke, the bodies, the burning...the pounding of hooves and the boots of men marching in the wrecked streets... cries of people screaming to be pulled from the rubble... tumbling bricks scattered by flaming missiles launched from hurlers. He remembered those things, and the terror of not being able to find his mother, and someone eventually snatching him and throwing him into a camp with thousands of people and no water, where he had stayed until Imrun needed a clerk. The camp commander had told him he had a boy who was very bright and had no parents and his future had been sealed, or so he had thought.

If he did not leave that day or the next, he never would. A return to the caravanserai guaranteed years of unhappiness, yoked against his will to a wife who didn't want him. Serafina might be compelled, but she would never consent.

Even so, his ties to her were stronger than she even knew. Serafina was still innocent; he was not. He wanted her, even if he had to trek through a desert to win her. But she would never give herself to him against her will. It was that fierce heart he loved. She had been a child when he came to Imrun and Hesta and he had humored her, playing hide and seek with her. She had always claimed it was too easy to find him and began to play the game blindfolded, challenging herself.

Now entering womanhood, she was still the same way.

"In here," he said, beckoning to her. The sounds and smell of the camel yard were unmistakable. Scores of animals stood or lay with their legs folded, secured by tethers attached to nose rings, eating precious hay to fortify them for long trips during which they would have only dried peas and barley to sustain them. They would drop huge amounts of weight before reaching Omana, where they would be better fed in order to make the return trip, and then they would endure it again. Some had done it many times. A lot of those were going to end as camel meat and hides. But there were others that might be worth purchase, and still others that already belonged to caravanners who would charge merchants for their use.

All of these were single humped camels, large and ornery, but they were able to carry immense loads as long as they reached water holes every hundred miles. Those who knew the location of those holes could command substantial fees for their guidance, but they needed younger men and boys for the work.

"We can either buy camels and sign on with a train or sign onto the train and use theirs," he advised her, low-voiced. "I suggest the latter. I have little experience with them and you have none. Save your money for when you reach Omana, if we do."

"If?"

He shrugged. "The desert is a harsh mistress. Some always die. Usually more the camels, but some men, also. And for a woman?"

He glanced sideways at her. "Very dangerous."

"Less so if you are with me," she replied.

He nodded, resigned. She was not proposing this for love him, or even because she understood that he needed freedom, too. Her mind was set. She wanted to learn who she was, and he only hoped she was not sorry if she did.

"Keep your money hidden," he warned her. "When I have secured us a place, I will use it to buy clothes and boots and bedrolls. The North will be cold. And bite off your nails. Your hands will give us away."

She nodded, thoughtfully. "I will."

He circumvented the yard, not making eye contact with anyone, while she trailed him dutifully. Finally, he halted in front of a deeply tanned, turbaned man with a bushy white beard. The color of both hair and skin bespoke decades of experience in the desert and he dressed in a striped caftan of a caravanner.

"Do you need more help for the road?" Jalal asked.

"First time?" the man inquired, astutely.

"Yes." Jalal gestured casually in Serafina's direction. "I have some experience, my brother has none, but he knows how to work."

It seemed this man could evaluate people as quickly as Jalal could. "That is what is required," he agreed. "We leave in the morning. Can you be ready?"

"We are ready right now," Jalal said, with quiet assurance.

"Good. What are your names?"

"I am Yusuf," he lied. "My brother is Ilfan."

It was likely they would be sought when they failed to return home and they must not be traced by their names. Besides, Ilfan was close enough to Serafina that she would probably respond to it quickly. The family had often called her Fina. Now and for the foreseeable future, she was Ilfan.

"I am Bazir," the older man said. "Bring clothing, bedrolls and good boots. I will feed you. Get canteens from my herder." He indicated another, slightly younger man lounging by the gate to the yard. "Drink well and be sure they are filled before we go. Come before dawn."

Jalal—now Yusuf—nodded, touching his forehead respectfully, and Serafina followed him silently to the gate, where the herder who had been watching their conversation handed them each a canteen. It was a sign that Bazir trusted them to return. He might not have, but something in Jalal's bearing had convinced him, apparently.

"Where will we sleep?" Serafina asked when they had stepped away.

"By the water," Jalal replied. "I have often slept on the beach. It is not bad if you shake off the little sand crabs that come out at night."

"Ugh," Serafina laughed. "Will you buy what we need?"

"Yes, it is better if I do." Jalal looked down at her feet. "Place your foot next to mine. I must see what size boots you will take."

Their calves touched through the thin cloth of their robes as she put her foot down for measuring. Her long, slim, high arched foot was two-thirds the size of his. Jalal looked at its imprint in the sand and smiled.

"Also get a length of cloth, something easily torn," Serafina advised. "And lambs wool."

Jalal didn't understand.

"I am a woman, you know," she said. "There are times I will need those."

It was his turn to look embarrassed. "And how will we disguise that part?"

"With difficulty, I am sure," she admitted. "I will find a way."

"All right," he replied. "First we will go to the beach. I will stake out a spot and you can hold it for us."

She looked at him quizzically.

"We will not be the only ones on the beach tonight. Others will join the caravan at dawn. I will return with food and supplies."

Understanding then, she nodded. Nothing on the coast near Someno was far from the beach and after only a short walk Jalal spotted a relatively private place behind a sandy hillock, where he left her.

When he had gone, Serafina glanced about nervously. She knew she would get little sleep that night, but she also knew she would have gotten none without Jalal. She would have had no idea what to do. Aside from that, it was getting dark and she knew Ummi would be growing concerned. Serafina had never stayed out past dark. As it fell, she knew her mother would think Imrun and Jalal had taken her and, though grieved, she would not be terrified. When it was learned that both of them were missing, though, that would be another story.

But she gave Jalal a bright smile when he returned with everything they needed and a meal of cheese and peppers grilled in chunks of bakoosh. It was the bread her mother's friend, Saleema, had brought to Jadda's funeral feast, signifying the start of a new life cycle.

She was starting her own. Perhaps it would all be in vain. She might perish in the desert or be turned back at the border. Even if they let her into Omana, the camel trains stopped there and she and Jalal would be on their own making their way halfway down the country to the capitol, Xanthus. And that was assuming he wanted to go so far. He might not or he might be regarded as dangerous and taken. He was Domidian—something they despised. Then what would she do?

Relieving herself behind the hillock, understanding then why he had chosen it, she let tears come.

CHAPTER 5

Jalal's touch on her shoulder wakened her the next morning. She had slept uneasily, disturbed by the sounds of the beach and the unrealized threat of sand crabs crawling on her. They had not bothered her, but the grittiness of the pervasive sand and inability to wash it off were uncomfortable. She could not go into the ocean to rinse and already she longed for a clean bed and warm water. Reluctantly, she sat up.

She could barely see Jalal's face in the pre-dawn darkness.

"I heard you crying last night," he said. "If you want to turn back, this is the time."

Determined, she shook her head. "No, I want to go. Just tell me what to do."

"First, eat," he replied, handing her bread and cheese. "Drink. I will refill our canteens from the public well. I bought extra, so that we can carry two each. It can save your life in the desert."

"How do you know these things?" She knew Jalal could never have spent time there. He was too busy jumping to obey Imrun's multitudinous orders.

"I have learned much by visiting these markets," he said. "Use some water to wash, behind the hillock. The sand will irritate your skin. Then I will get more."

She knew she would not often have the chance and made haste to follow his instructions, evading detection in the dark and then robing herself again quickly. Returning, she simply handed her canteen to him and watched as he set off up the beach to pursue every available drop before they left.

He was not gone long. She had packed up their improvised camp by the time he returned, thoroughly shaking and rolling their bedrolls and strapping their packs securely.

"Good," he said. "Give me one, then turn around."

She did as he asked and he fitted the shoulder straps over her arms, then hung two full canteens around her neck, one in front, the other in back. They were heavy, but she knew they probably would not be for long. As soon as he had done the same, he just said, "Come."

Obediently, not feeling much like talking, she followed him in semi-darkness to the camel yard. Her heart was pounding with anxiety. In a scant hour or so, she would be leaving Someno forever. She had never been outside its confines.

The herder, Elazeer, met them and the others in a group. For the first time, Serafina was within a group of men and boys, saying nothing as she hung by Jalal's side.

"You younger ones," Elazeer instructed, "you will lead the camels to water. It is there." He gestured to a large open cistern. "These two..." and he gestured to assistants, "will show you older ones how to load them when they have watered."

He smiled, white teeth flashing in the darkness. "Camels know when you are new or afraid. They will try to bite or throw up cud on you. It seems to amuse them. Do not show fear, but do not abuse them, because they will not forget it and will look for the chance to injure you. Simply step aside, do not let go of their tether, and they will follow their leaders. They are only testing you."

Giving Jalal a sardonic look, Serafina joined the younger group. There were six of them, boys her age or only slightly older, excited and teasing each other. Now, her speech would be tested.

"I am Hagid," one introduced himself. He was not as tall as Serafina, she noted with some amusement. Many men and boys were not. One thing she liked about Jalal was that he was taller. Her father had imparted height to her, by all accounts. That and her green eyes betrayed her heritage, but the fact that she was a woman was the real danger.

"Ilfan," she replied, pitching her voice carefully.

"You are here with your brother?"

"Yes, but he is older," she replied. "He has gone with the others."

"You are lucky to have a companion," he said. "I am alone here."

"You have no family?"

"Too many. If I leave, they have one less to feed."

She just nodded, still not trusting herself to speak too much. Fortunately, after that there was no chance. The two assistants directed them to camels. Hers, thankfully, was standing. Wisps of hay dropped from his mouth as he chewed slowly, looking as if the act claimed his full attention. Even when she detached his rope from his post, he paid her no heed. Some of the others were groaning, being urged to their feet, or spitting because they didn't like being interrupted.

"You know, don't you?" Serafina said softly to her camel, rubbing gently into his neck with her knuckles. At the touch, he simply swung his head around, apparently evaluating her with his topaz-colored eyes. "You must have done this many times. Come on, let's get you a drink."

It was intimidating, having something that large and potentially dangerous padding behind you like an oversized dog, but he followed in a line to the cistern, edging into place to claim his share of water.

"Does this one have a name?" Serafina asked the assistant, but he just shrugged.

"Call him what you like."

He spoke to the boys at large. "Each camel is assigned to you. They do not like changes in their caretakers, so become familiar with them. But it is always possible you must handle another at some point, so learn. They take their water slowly. They may drink three or four times. That water must carry them for a hundred miles, so let them finish. Then return them where you see the older men, who will load them."

"What do they carry?" one boy asked.

"Only our supplies, for now," the man replied. "We will travel days north to the salt mines. That is where the real loading begins. From there it is north to the border with Omana, where wagons will take the salt the rest of the way."

Perhaps there would be a way to get a ride south in Omana, Serafina thought with a surge of hope.

"They do not let our camels in," the assistant explained. "What grass they have, they keep for their own animals. The camels would compete, so they let us graze them on our side of the border and then send them back with the things they sell us."

He laughed. "By then, you will know them well. We will leave once the sun is up."

It was like filling a whale, Serafina thought, watching her charge drink at his leisure. That water would nourish his hump, though, making him an invaluable asset in conditions that would kill a horse. Horses were afraid of the camels, anyway, and she could not say that she blamed them. Hers had been docile so far, but she was sure if he was angry or frightened, it could be another story.

"Come," she finally said to him, when it appeared he was finished. With luck, she could find Jalal to load him and they could at least start their journey together. Behind them, Someno would disappear into the sunrise, and she might never see it or anyone else she knew ever again. This could be the price of her freedom. She wondered if she could pay it, but then she thought again of Jadda, small and lonely in her grave. Even if it ended in disaster, she would not live her life that way.

* * *

SHE HAD EXPECTED SAND DUNES, but to her surprise the land they traversed at first was simply dry and gravelly, with a few desiccated-looking low trees and brush the camels sometimes tried to grab if it seemed edible. It wasn't, Jalal told her, but it would be helpful for starting campfires. Cooler now that it was not summer, the desert permitted them the luxury of traveling in early morning and late afternoon, and sometimes well into the night before they finally stopped to make camp. They needed the fires then and she watched the men digging pits, piling in brush plus tinder and firewood the camels carried, then using a fire board and stick to produce sawdust that eventually smoldered and caught with the brush.

"They are happy, aren't they?" she asked Jalal quietly one night, sitting just outside the nimbus of warmth the fire produced. Others depended on it, but Jalal had bought heavy robes and blankets that paid for themselves many times over as the temperature plunged at night. Less foresighted men sat or lounged near the flames or took shelter in hide lean-tos that would be dismantled in the morning, being used for shelter once more in the strongest heat of the day, when they fended off the sun.

"They are free here," he responded, eating the ground beans and olive oil on bread that everyone took. To Serafina's surprise, there was ample water and tea and the more experienced men encouraged them to drink, telling them not to wait until they felt thirst. The camels carried numerous barrels and skins of water and there were a lot of them. It was not a small caravan and Jalal told her that was safer. They could last until the first water hole or oasis better than a smaller one could. It was why he had chosen it.

He gestured to the star-spangled sky. "Where else would you see this? Not in the city. The men cooperate because they will perish without each other. There is no place for fighting. The work is hard, but there is peace."

"True," she agreed.

They were both children of war, Jalal even more than she was. No wonder he sought peace.

"I have already learned a lot," she commented.

Beside her, he nodded. "You handle the camel well and you work hard. I believe Bazir is coming to appreciate your value. He just doesn't know it comes from a woman."

She laughed cautiously. "Yes, if he knew, he would think I was going to faint and have to be carried to Omana on one of his camels."

"You will not faint," Jalal replied, still eating. His tone was neutral, but she sensed he meant it as a compliment.

No, she would not. She worked tirelessly every day, without complaint. She had even passed her first moon time without incident and without letting any of the men learn of it. She suspected Jalal knew because he covered for her, often asking her to go off alone to gather brush and tinder so that she could attend to her needs in private. When she showed no sign of suffering, he showed her no extra courtesy, either. He treated her like he did the others. Everyone knew she was supposedly his brother, but no one could accuse him of favoritism. She found she missed it, just a bit.

It even occurred to her—with a sense of deep irony—that the very person she had tried to escape was now with her. She had not escaped him at all.

She studied him surreptitiously by firelight. He was not bad-looking, with a high, intelligent forehead, prominent cheekbones and an aquiline nose, not overly large as so many were. Imrun looked like he was being led around by his. Her mother's cousin's beard was scraggly, too, whereas Jalal somehow contrived to keep his trimmed. It was jet black, like his hair, and his hands were well formed and capable. The bone structure of his face was very fine, lending an appearance of mysticism to his eyes, which were dark and eloquent.

It was small wonder he was drawn to the desert. This was not a man who would ever have made a merchant.

She sighed to herself. It was a pity she could not love him.

CHAPTER 6

Onward they trudged. One day was pretty much like another, punctuated only by her grief for her mother. Ummi must have lost hope by now, she thought, though she was no longer sure just how long they had been traveling. The duties were routine and never-ending. Wake up, eat short rations, feed the camel, walk him for miles, pause at mid-day for rest, put up a shelter, take down a shelter, then walk more miles. The camel was not for her convenience. Like her, he was there to work, and she led him.

"How far is it to the mines?" she asked Jalal, walking with him once more. It was his job to load the camel with great care and continually ensure that the load remained intact. Their very existence hinged on it, and his training from Imrun stood him in good stead. Jalal never shirked any duties, he never complained, he was level-headed and steady. She could tell that Bazir liked him, sometimes deigning to share their place at the campfire as he almost never did with any of the younger men. She could sense the caravanner felt Jalal might be another one in the making and so gave him extra attention.

"I don't know," he replied. "Those who have made the trip said we will pass through a land of dunes and wadis and that it will become more difficult before we reach the mines."

"Difficult how?" she wondered. They had already circumvented wadis that looked like good pathways, but when she had suggested they might find an easier path there, Jalal had shaken his head.

"There are mountains north and west," he said. "They get rain in this season, even though we do not see it here. When it comes down those wadis, it can wipe away any train caught in it. When the waters subside a little, all the creatures that want it come out—snakes, scorpions, lizards, spiders as big as your hand."

He looked at her with a smile. "Shake out your bedroll each morning. Boots, too. Never put your hand on top of a rock without looking first. Snakes like to sun themselves there."

"I saw a fox," she noted, and he looked at her with interest.

"Where?"

"Oh, it was this morning. Very small, with big ears."

"Tell me if you see another. It may be hunting something we can use." The men brought in anything they could hunt as they moved, in order to supplement the rations they carried. A desert hare or birds' eggs would be very welcome.

He put a hand almost casually on their camel's neck. Serafina had never named the beast, but he seemed to like her, if it was possible to discern a camel's preferences, and he tolerated Jalal.

"Can you knit?"

The question was totally unexpected, but she nodded.

"Pull some of the longer hairs from his neck when we camp at night and wind it into twine. Knit some masks. You know how, don't you?"

"Won't they know then I'm a woman?"

"No, the men do it, too, since there are no women here. Well, not usually, anyway. Borrow some needles from them. Once we are in the dunes, sand will fill up masks so quickly it will be impossible to have enough."

It sounded ominous, but she had known they would go there. They had to in order to reach the mines. "All right."

He said nothing more, but their campfire that night was no longer of wood curls and twigs. Instead, the boys had been sent to collect dried camel dung left by previous caravans. It littered the land in telltale clumps, denoting a time-worn path trod by hundreds.

Bringing back her share that night, she dumped it alongside the communal fire centered among their shelters. On the outer perimeter of the camp, hobbled camels stood or lay chewing what rations could be spared for them, their occasional grunts and wheezing complaints echoing in the stillness. The smoke of their dung hung in the night air. Above that, stars shone with the brilliance of diamonds in the desert night. Relieved of her load, Serafina took her accustomed place beside Jalal, who was beside Bazir, both of them speaking quietly. Saying nothing, she pulled out a bag of the camel's hair, wet her fingers in her mouth and began twining it just as some of the men were doing. Even she had begun to see changes in the land and wondered if she could fashion masks before they reached the dunes, but Bazir nodded approvingly.

"You will need those," he said. "Work them each night, as long as you can before you sleep."

It was going to be a sacrifice. Sleep was something she sought like a drug, her bedroll only a short distance from Jalal's. She was exhausted not only from her work and walking every day, but also from the distress of leaving her mother. It seemed to Serafina she missed her more each day as distance increasingly separated them, yet she knew it was pointless. She had chosen this, after all, and no doubt Pescia suffered far more than she did. The only comfort her mother might have was the supposition that she was with Jalal. She wondered if she could somehow contrive to get a message to her from Omana. Her mother was able to read, if only a little, because it helped her in the market.

"I will," she promised, twining industriously.

Bazir gifted her with one of his rare smiles. "You have done well for us, Ilfan. And your brother, I think, could be one of us."

Jalal said nothing, not committing himself. Serafina knew that was not his dream, yet he would not be discourteous to Bazir, who had been kind and was watching both of them, his gaze shrewd.

"You are not born of the same father, are you?" he asked, but it was not a question.

Fortunately, Jalal was quick-witted.

"No," he improvised. "I was born before the war, Ilfan after. After the Havacians had come."

Bazir made a soft noise of mixed understanding and disgust. Serafina had heard it before.

"So many of our women were dishonored," he said.

"It is not my brother's fault," Jalal replied at once.

"No, of course not," Bazir half apologized. "I did not say so."

Once, Serafina might have been offended. Now, she felt only relief because it was her Havacian blood the caravanner had recognized, not the fact that she was female.

"Does your father live?" he asked Jalal.

"No, he was killed in the war."

"I am sorry." Bazir spared Serafina a sympathetic glance. "Sorry for you, also."

She could not say that her father was alive, of course, or

that he appeared to be at least somewhat decent, having supported her for five-and- ten years. No doubt her mother would continue taking his money. It was the least he owed her.

"Well, consider a future in the caravans, if you wish," Bazir said, "or you may find attractions in Omana."

Jalal looked up at him, clearly surprised, and the older man laughed.

"I have lost promising young men to Omana before. Domidia will never prosper under their rule. Better to eat from the hand of your enemy than to starve. But better yet the freedom of the desert."

"Perhaps," Jalal said, non-committal.

Bazir rose, resting a hand on his shoulder briefly. "We have many miles to go. Take your time."

Serafina looked at Jalal from under her lashes when he had gone. "He would take you on, I think."

He stretched his legs to the fire, betraying no emotion. "Probably."

"But it is not what you want?"

"I am not sure," he confessed. "It would mean a life on the road most of each year, leaving behind whatever or whoever was important to me."

"But the money is good," she pointed out. Bazir had been generous to them, considering their lack of experience.

"Money is not everything."

Jalal sounded enigmatic, not revealing what was in his mind.

"You still want horses?" she pressed. Domidia, once home of some of the world's finest mounts, would never have them again under the Omanis, who took every precaution to see Domidia could not make war again. For horses, one had to go to Omana or beyond. She had no idea what lay beyond, although she supposed Jalal might know. Men got a few years of schooling, though women did not.

"Perhaps." He would only answer her in a circular fashion, Serafina realized. The conversation could not really go anywhere and she was growing tired.

"Well, they breed them in Omana," she said, pushing her knitting into the bag she had carried to the fire. "I am going to sleep."

"Are you angry with me?"

"No. I just don't know what you want."

"We are not all as single-minded as you," he responded. The men had mainly drifted off to their bedrolls, leaving them some measure of privacy. "If you are interested, I will let you know when I make up my mind."

She stood up. "Good. You should talk to somebody."

"Why?"

"Because it is good to have somebody to talk to."

He didn't answer and she went the short distance to her bedroll, shaking it carefully before she removed her boots and crawled into it, starting to toss her bag of knitting under her head for a pillow, then thinking better of it. Her needles were borrowed. It would not do to break them. Instead, she shoved her boots under her head with a faint shudder of disgust. At least her hair would not be dirty, since she wore a turban. There was no water to spare for washing it. Perhaps if one of those wadis filled, there would be.

It was her last, hopeful thought for the night.

HER WISHES WERE MORE powerful than she thought. They had been traveling for only a short distance the next morning when she heard a warning cry from the head of the line: "Water comes!"

Immediately, the men turned their animals to the left, uphill away from the wadi, prodding and even whipping them as they seldom did so that they broke into a lumbering canter.

"Wait!" Jalal called to her urgently, so that she turned to see what he wanted. In two strides, he had caught up with her and was hoisting her onto the camel, where she clung breathlessly to the straps that tied down his load. She had never ridden him before, but then she had never needed to. It felt like an earthquake beneath her as Jalal ran full tilt beside him, urging him to higher ground.

From her vantage point atop the tall animal, she could see the first churn of water down the wadi. Any thought of bathing in it disappeared at once. It was a viscous muddy brown, frothing and carrying rocks and branches in its tide, washing up and over the sides of the narrow channel as they clambered desperately up ground hopefully high enough to escape it. She heard the voices of men and the groaning protest of camels above its noise, but everything seemed to be happening in a haze.

Visibly panting and shaken, Jalal ran up an embankment with the camel's tether clutched in his hand. They could go no further; it would either be high enough or it would not. Frozen in fear, Serafina watched the water ripping down the wadi, tunneling out the sides, pooling on the higher ground. It stopped mere feet away, forming a torrent below them. Beneath her, she could feel the camel's flanks shuddering. He was clearly as much aware of the danger as they were. And yet people called them dumb beasts.

"You're all right, you're all right," she murmured, as much to herself as to him.

Jalal looked up, his expression strained. "It will pass us. Just stay there."

Bazir was pacing the line, counting men and camels,

examining the loads. The water roared on, a mindless force impervious to their existence.

"It's good," Serafina heard him calling to the men. "Wait here for it to pass. It may take some time."

"All right, you can get down now," Jalal told her, putting a hand against her back as she lowered herself, holding to the camel's front girth.

She looked at him gratefully, steadying herself on the ground. "That was close."

"Not as much as it might have been," he replied. The camel was lowering himself to the ground, refusing to go any further, but as long as he did not roll on his load, neither of them tried to stop him. He had earned his rest. Unstrapping one of their packs, Serafina reached in to fill her hand with dried dates, which she gave him. The offer was accepted immediately, disappearing into the vast cavern of his mouth where he ground the treat with obvious relish, jaws working.

"You will make a dog of him yet," Jalal said. "You should drink."

Mouth dry with fear, she slung her canteen to drink, happy that he had reminded her of it.

"You, too," she said, but unnecessarily. He was already opening his own.

"That was good," she said. "I would not have thought of getting on him."

Jalal just shrugged. "He was higher than the waters and stronger than we are. It was the safest place for you."

Not for him, though, she thought. Jalal could easily have drowned, but he had protected her first. She remembered his touch as he helped her down. It had not been unwelcome. She no longer felt half fearful of him, away from Imrun's pressure and Ummi's tacit agreement. Here, they were more partners.

If only they had not tried to force him on her, she thought, it might have been different.

"Does it last long?"

He shrugged. "I don't know. I never saw one before, I just knew they could happen. We won't try to cross, in any event."

She nodded. Bazir, wise in the way of the trail, had kept them going parallel to the wadi on the side where they could reach higher ground. On the other side, they would still have been washed away. Even the camel's additional height would not have saved her then.

In the end, he decided to camp for the day, even though it was unusual. Serafina was grateful, sensing the uneasy cramping of her moon tide coming, by which she knew that they had traveled for two months. She was not sick, just uncomfortable, and nervous about concealing her condition.

This time, she knew Jalal saw her take her knitting bag in which she also carried what was necessary. But when she did not begin to knit, he opened his own bag, pulling out a slingshot and handing it to her.

"Here," he said, loudly enough for anyone interested to hear. "See if you can find the hare that fox was hunting. I will stay with the camel."

She just nodded as if being sent out for the hunt. He had shown her the use of a sling, which she had learned rapidly. It was even possible she might catch dinner.

"You cook it if I catch it," she told him, cheekily. "Don't fall asleep."

CHAPTER 7

She caught nothing, because there was nothing to catch. All the desert creatures seemed to have disappeared. Not even sand trap spiders tunneled into their holes at her approach. It was growing noticeably cooler. She found the change welcome, but once she had made a cursory circle well outside of their makeshift camp, there was nothing left to do, so she retraced her steps. They had not yet entered the trackless dunes where everyone but the most experienced risked becoming lost. She could still spot enough landmarks to make her way back.

Their camp was merely a line of hide shelters and drowsing camels prostrate on the earth, like a row of teeth sticking up from the ground. There was nothing else but the occasional bush and weeds sometimes rolling in a tangled web the camels tried to avoid, since it entrapped their long legs.

"Have they decided not to work today?" she laughed, returning to Jalal. He was standing beside their camel and had erected a shelter.

"I don't know," he mused. Ordinarily, about half the

camels stood while the others lay down and slept. Serafina supposed it was how they survived in the wild, posting a guard of sorts. Now, all were down.

"Well, I didn't catch anything," she said, still jovial. The thought of resting for a day had made her giddy with relief.

"It doesn't matter," he replied absently, scanning the horizon.

"What are you looking for?"

"Clouds."

"Why should there be clouds?" Thus far, the desert sky had been a huge blue bowl burning them by day and freezing them by night.

"There was rain," he said. "West of us. That is where the flood came from."

"So?" She strapped her bag back on the camel, who did not even crack an eyelid.

"There is ocean to the west," he said, "though it is many miles away. That is where the rain comes at this time of the year, and lightning."

Serafina knew that. Thunderstorms on the coast had occasionally terrified her; she had been grateful they did not come in the desert. Their train had seemed to be heading roughly northeast, away from such things.

"Those breezes meet with the desert."

She still didn't understand. "If they make it cooler, I am grateful."

He laughed in a way that was not amused. "You shouldn't be. That is what makes the haboob."

Abruptly, her heart plummeted. The monumental sandstorms had not much troubled them in Someno. She could remember only two: howling demons that had spurred both her mother and grandmother to terror, sheltering her under blankets in the apartment while sand swept the caravanserai like something loosed from hell. Many things and even people had been buried afterwards. There had been disastrous damage and some whose lungs were weak perished. Even the word struck fear.

"A haboob?" she asked. "Here?"

"Maybe." He was still scanning the sky to the west, where flat gray clouds seemed to be hovering, blocking sunlight, although the sky ahead of it was still blue.

"I do not like the look of it," he said. "I heard the men discussing it. They are uneasy, too. And the camels are not behaving normally."

"Animals often know things we do not," Serafina agreed, and he nodded.

"They do. I know they curl in balls during the storms with their noses down, trying not to breathe sand. They are lying that way now."

"What do we do?" She did not mind ceding authority to Jalal when he knew more than she did.

"Wait for Bazir to instruct us. I am sure he will. But if worse comes to worst, lie against the camel. He will not move during the storm. Use all your masks and cover yourself until it is over."

"Where will you be?"

Dark eyes glinting, he scanned the perimeter, finding no one who could overhear. "Right on top of you."

That wrung a laugh from her, despite her fear.

"You're a good man, Jalal," she told him.

"Really?" he replied, with an edge of sarcasm. *Not good enough for you, though,* that tone said. "I said I would come, and I did. That is all. Your chances of surviving this trip are not good without help. I told you, the desert is a harsh mistress."

"Is that why you came?"

"Partly." His tone was still flat, as if simply giving her reasons. She had hurt his pride with her refusal of marriage and he was not yet ready to forgive or understand it, though he would not force her. The need to do that would have been even more offensive.

"Put a halter on the camel," he went on. "Tuck the cloth from your pack through the noseband and let it hang. It will make a mask for him. Give him some barley to keep him busy. Eat and drink, get some sleep if you can. I will keep watch. Bazir will look out for us, too. He is surely no fool about these things."

It was cool enough now to wrap herself in a blanket, so after she had tended to the camel she did, lying inside the hide shelter, searching her conscience. She did not care if she hurt Imrun with her behaviors. He was a wretched little rat who cared for nothing but his own prosperity. But Ummi and Jalal? They had not deserved what she was putting them both through.

Eventually, though, the quiet of the desert lulled her and she slept.

* * *

IT WAS NOT Jalal who wakened her, but Hagid. He had been friendly to her the way the young boys were with each other, but she had not encouraged the friendship, too concerned with being discovered as a woman.

"Ilfan, wake up," he said, squatting beside the shelter.

She sat up promptly, remembering what Jalal had told her. "What is it?"

"Bazir says to make ready for a storm."

So, it had come, then. Peering to the west, she could see totally incongruous blue sky towering above a menacing red-brown wall that looked as if it was boiling inside.

"Where is Yusuf?" she asked at once. It came hard, using Jalal's assumed name, but even then she did not forget.

"With the others," Hagid replied. "Making the camp ready. You should take your shelter down, it will only blow away and you will be left without it."

"The gods help us," she said, watching the oncoming monster.

"Gods can't help this," Hagid said, with a grim practicality. "Crawl in with your camel, throw the shelter over you and lay on it. Use your masks. I must go now."

"Yes, go," she urged.

Getting up, he ran to where she could see figures of the other men, their robes and pants billowing in the oncoming wind, busily dismantling shelters and securing camels. The animals showed no inclination to move, however, and Serafina quickly realized she could indeed use hers as a living bulwark against the storm. Thankful that she had always been good to him and he seemed to bear her no ill will, she donned masks and dismantled the shelter with shaking fingers. The light seemed to be disappearing, blotted out by the encroaching storm. Despite Hagid's doubts, she prayed.

There still was no sign of Jalal as she crawled beneath the hides she had taken down, drawing them around her beside the shelter of the camel's body. For just a moment, he sniffed at her as if ensuring it was the human he knew, then uttered a long groan, settling himself more firmly.

Too terrified to attempt to look out, she felt the first blast of air, huddling with her face close to the earth. It was more imperative to stay sheltered until the moment she felt the hide tugged and moved aside so that Jalal could slide in.

"It comes," he said, unnecessarily, because she could hear the wind howling and feel things pelting her. "Head down."

Wrapping both of them in a leather cocoon, he pressed hard against her, arms around her, pulling her face to his chest. She was shaking and felt his hands on her back and his arms holding her fast against the wind.

"No more talk," he said. "Keep your mouth closed."

It was on them then, the howling monster she remembered from her childhood. Memory reawakened, she lay paralyzed with fear the same as she had done then, wrapped in a rug with her mother and grandmother holding her down. Now it was Jalal holding her, unable to speak, simply putting his body between hers and the storm, offering himself as a sacrifice. When this was over, she thought, she must make it up to him, somehow.

It had been normal for them to grow apart as they aged. She could not forever play hide and seek with him...yet she had. Now he sought her as a man and she had been blind, as blind as she had been then, just in a different way. As a child, she had worn a blindfold. As a woman, she had used a mask of indifference and rejection.

She wanted to say something to him...to apologize, perhaps...but it was impossible to speak against the howl of the storm. His body spoke for him. She could feel him hard against her thigh, aroused by the feel of her body through her thin robe.

Panting and gasping with the sand seeping in despite many masks, she had no words. It was entirely possible they would die. The camel could be covered. He could suffocate. He was not moving and she had no idea whether he was dead or alive. She was inside the belly of the beast in every way: engulfed by the storm, her only shields the body of the camel and the raw desire of the man whose embrace defended her. She moved against him, holding him close.

She had denied him because she had felt no choice in the matter. There was a choice now, if they both lived.

* * *

It seemed like forever, but eventually things stopped hitting her and she felt the camel stir. She and Jalal were both choking and retching, clawing at their masks, which now were no comfort, making them feel even more suffocated.

"Gah!" Jalal sat up beside her, spitting without apology. Choking on grit, she did the same while he threw back the sand-weighted cover over them. She doubted she could have done it, it was so heavy, and stared around them in shock.

The world was white, the sand glowing with a gelatinous mass of stones stretching to the horizon.

"Hail," Jalal said. "The haboob has brought it down out of the sky."

Serafina just stared at it, disbelieving. "Is that snow?" No one in Someno had ever seen snow.

"Hail," he repeated. "Somewhat the same. It is what you felt hitting us."

"I did at that," she said, but then turned her attention to the camel, who was standing up, shaking himself like the dog Jalal always threatened he could become. Annoyed, he tossed his head to rid himself of the cone of material Serafina had rigged inside his noseband, trying to help him breathe.

"Wait, wait," she told him, as if he could understand, reaching up and relieving him of his burden. Sometimes she suspected he did understand her in a dim sort of way. In any case, he was never nasty with her as some of the camels were and now she scratched his face gently, thanking him for his protection.

Jalal hauled himself up by the carry straps, pushing sand off the camel's load in a tremendous shower. They were not as deeply buried as they would have been in the dunes, but it was imperative their cargo not be damaged. All their food and water rode on the camels. Anxiously, he uncorked their water bladder, taking a tentative sip and then spitting it out with a sound of disgust. Cork or no, it had been contaminated.

"Oh, no," Serafina said softly, understanding at once. "How far to the next water hole?"

"I don't know," Jalal confessed, sliding down again. "And if it is an open cistern, it may be sand-filled."

"If it is a well?" she asked anxiously.

"Better. We may still be able to sieve the water through a cloth." He nodded to the piece of fabric she had taken from the camel. "Keep that. We will need it."

She just nodded, watching Bazir's approaching figure.

"Are you ready to move?" he asked.

Jalal nodded. "Is anyone lost?"

"No, but we must go quickly. Only half our water can be drunk. What is in the wadi is useless. It would probably kill us. I know of a water hole where the water must be drawn up and we can most likely use it, but everyone else will be going there, too."

Jalal just nodded, tightening the camel's straps. The animal stood patiently, a monument to survival. Whether or not the humans could survive was now an open question. Serafina had an unpleasant mental image of their prone figures lying in the sand while herds of now-wild camels returned to the desert that had made them, untroubled by their demise. It was humans who took them from their place and made them carry burdens all their lives, never resting, always serving. And then they ate them, when they were too old to serve.

If their camel had saved them, it was merely an accident.

She looked anxiously and a bit speculatively at Jalal, preparing to depart. If he saved her, it would be no accident. She remembered the feel of his body against hers, marveling that at the moment of imminent death he had still been aroused. It was what men did, she supposed. She would not make more of it than it was or embarrass him by mentioning it. Privy to the sometimes incautious language of Ummi and her friends, she knew exactly how that worked. They could be aroused by anything even remotely female. It wasn't even necessarily about her, although in Jalal's case she was uneasily aware that it probably was.

But she couldn't think about that. She was not much of a woman—too tall, without curves, with strange eyes and too many opinions. Women should be submissive. She never had been. It was exactly why she was about to be in the middle of the desert, far from everything she had ever known except him.

CHAPTER 8

Now she realized their trip thus far had been leisurely, compared to what followed.

Everyone in the area would have been caught in the haboob. All water was damaged unless it was underground. Those who reached it first would live.

This was how so many had perished in the war with Havacia and the Omanis, when their cisterns had been destroyed. Ummi had told her about it many times, and how Imrun and her Havacian lover had saved her when so many others had died.

There was no one to save Serafina unless the men of the caravan could do it. Now, she saw them spurred to grim purpose in a race to the oasis.

Sand from the haboob was everywhere, layering everything in such a thick blanket that she nearly did not notice, at first, when they passed from arid scrub brush to true dunes. The flat feet of their camels were invaluable, traversing the ground at three times the speed of a man, and most often everyone rode, squished in among the cargo, but since it was dwindling at an alarming rate, after a time that didn't matter.

Now she began to see towering dunes above her, one after the other, indistinguishable except to Bazir as they crawled like ants up the vast sweep of sand that changed with every errant breeze. Fickle whirlwinds danced about them as if challenging their passage. Devils of the desert, people called them.

"How does he know where we are?" she asked Jalal several days out. Both of them rode the camel, one ahead of the cargo, one behind. Lacking each other's support, they grasped whatever they could to stay on him.

"It is the color of the sand, he says." Jalal answered over the noise of the caravan snaking its way between dunes or around the tops. Daytime shelter from the sun was a thing of the past, as were many hours of sleep at night. Bazir guided them then by the stars, which looked close enough to touch. The dazzling display would have enchanted Serafina if she had not known they were running for their lives. There was no water for the camels and little for the humans. She did not have to be told this was when some died and, if they did, there was no time to stop for them. Their bones would litter the sand, to be covered by the next haboob.

She was gritty, dirty, often hungry, and exhausted. The days no longer mattered; she had lost track of them. Weight dropped off her just as it did from the camel. Jalal seemed to fare somewhat better, often giving her a share of his food and water to keep her going. His darker complexion protected him better from the sun and Serafina, who had always prided herself on her will, began to suspect his exceeded it. He was tireless, saying little, but never stopping in a determined fight to survive.

She had made a friend in Hagid, too, who often came to check on her, though she didn't know why. Fearing discovery, she had made no overtures to him, and she thought it might be only that they were close in age and he missed his family. Yet if he brought her an extra sip of water or a spare ration, she was happy enough to take it.

The caravan, she realized, was no place for pride. It beat it out of her, day after relentless day.

At last, the land began to level out and Bazir encouraged the men, saying they were drawing near the oasis where water inexplicably flowed from the ground and a settlement had sprung up accordingly.

"Where does it come from?" she asked Jalal, who had finally dropped from the camel and proceeded on foot although he told her to ride.

"I think there must be underground rivers," he said, "and where the earth grows thin, they sometimes emerge. Bazir says this one is sizeable and there should be water and merchandise to replenish our supplies. At least, we hope so."

"We will have competition?" she guessed.

"Yes, and we must somehow procure enough to continue on to the salt mines, or else turn back. And that is not without danger, as well. Caravans do not usually turn back. They make the trip or die."

She shivered apprehensively.

"We can get more at the mines?"

He nodded. "Exactly. What we take on there must last until we reach the border. But it is not as far as we have already come."

Well, that was encouraging...she hoped.

"No more dunes?"

"No, we have passed them and most of the mountains. There will be only hills to get through, and then we will reach Omana." She knew he spoke every night to Bazir, learning these things. Though she might sit at camp fire with the men, she spoke very little, still wary of being discovered. If she did not mingle with the other boys, they put it down to the fact that she traveled with her brother. Jalal was unmistakably protective of her, though they thought it was because he was older and saw it as his duty, especially given that some might abuse her as a child of war.

Finally...finally...the graceful silhouette of palm trees and the outline of red clay walls announced they had reached their haven. When she could make out the figures of sheep and goats, Serafina knew there was water.

"Hiya," Bazir greeted the headman of the village. Riding at the front of their column, he was first to see everyone and apparently knew them well.

"You survived the storm!" the other man replied.

"Without incident." Bazir spoke as if their nightmare had never happened. "And you?"

"Not bad," the headman said. "I have not often seen hail, but we were spared for the most part."

"You have water, then?"

"Plenty." Her heart gave a great leap of relief and she smiled down triumphantly at Jalal. "There must have been powerful storms to the west. Our wells are flowing."

So, perhaps Jalal was right and this bounty sprang from rivers that somehow ran underground from the mountains, downhill to the southern tip of Domidia. Everyone knew such rivers ran the length of Omana, although above ground in their case. They were said to have more water than they even needed—one reason Domidia had invaded and conquered them.

But that had been before she was born. Now she must make her way there, hoping the traditional enmity had subsided enough for her to find information about her father. In all likelihood, he had returned to Havacia. But she wanted to know who he was—whose height and appearance and daunting personality she had inherited. Those things did not come from Ummi.

Women and children from the village were coming to

greet them, wearing the flowing caftans that helped to cool them. Serafina jumped down from the camel the way the boys did, anxious to lead him to water. They appeared to be the first caravan that had arrived and men were already drawing up water, dumping it into long troughs for the camels to drink. The animals pushed forward eagerly, in some cases dragging handlers along. Serafina was one of them.

"Oof," she protested as the camel barreled forward to where he could smell water. She just watched longingly as he pushed his nose into the bounty, wanting nothing more than to leap into one of the troughs, but she couldn't. Wet robes would outline her body.

Hagid came up behind her with his camel, grinning.

"Jump in!" he said.

"And be eaten by a camel?" She laughed, but noted other boys were doing exactly what Hagid suggested. Everyone was laughing and circling, excited and relieved by their survival and the promise of some comforts. Oh, the gods, how she longed for a bath.

"Hold my camel?" he asked.

"Sure." She took his mount's tether. Along with the other boys, he leaped into a second trough, sputtering. Only she stood with animals in her charge while women around her joined in the fun. The camel boys were hardly older than their own children.

One of them smiled at her. "Come to my house, and I will give you bakoosh. You are skinny as a plucked chicken!"

Serafina smiled at her gratefully. "Which one?"

The motherly woman gestured to one of the square clay cottages. They all looked alike, so Serafina marked it carefully.

"You come, when the camel is tethered," she insisted. "Your mother would not like to see you so skinny and dirty."

"No, she wouldn't," Serafina agreed. "I will come, thank you."

She could not ask if Jalal could come; he had not been invited. Perhaps she could take food back to him. But as soon as Hagid returned, taking both camels from her, she excused herself and followed the scent of food to the modest cottage.

"Come in, come in," the owner invited when she paused politely in the doorway, giving time to be noticed. "I am Dijaya, these are my children." She gestured to a band of dark-eyed imps. "My husband, I think, is busy selling to your caravan, but come and eat. We have plenty."

Shyly, Serafina took an indicated place at their long, low table. The children crowded around her, intent on eating. Dijaya promptly ladled out a stew of eggplant, tomatoes and peppers with onions—the best food Serafina had seen in months—and gestured to a basket of fresh-baked bakoosh while she poured precious water.

"Ack!" she reprimanded her children as they started to gobble. "Give thanks."

Piously, the whole table bent heads while their mother intoned, "Thanks be to the gods who give to us, and for a guest come to our door."

"Thank you," Serafina said. "This looks so good."

"I hope so." Dijaya passed her the bread basket. "Perhaps when you are done you would like to use our wash tub."

She gave Serafina a penetrating look. "I understand why you will not wish to bathe with the boys."

Serafina could feel herself coloring. Had she failed to deceive another woman?

Apparently.

"You are very brave," Dijaya said, speaking over the racket of her children, who were now paying no attention. "You came with your man in the caravan?"

Serafina could only nod, dumbly. Jalal was not exactly her

man, but it would never occur to this woman that she would be without one. She could see Dijaya glance quickly at her hand for a marriage band, but even when she didn't see one, she remained kind.

"I will give you a plate for him," her benefactress went on. "I will give you our tub and water and you can wash in the children's bedroom. Shall I send one of them to get a clean robe for you? I know Bazir well. He will pay. He will not mind."

"A boy's robes," Serafina half whispered, and Dijaya nodded.

"Of course. We will not give you away. But be careful."

"I have been," Serafina assured her.

"No, you be careful," the other woman insisted. "It is very rough at the mines. Very bad men, some of them. You are wise to travel as a boy. And do not get with child between here and the salt mines. It is a hard trip back."

"I am not going back, anyway."

"Ah, you try your luck in Omana?" Dijaya mopped up juice with her bakoosh, never missing a beat. "Your parents did not wish you to marry?"

It was a common reason for couples to run away.

"Something like that," Serafina mumbled.

Dijaya clucked sympathetically. "Well, many try for Omana."

"What do you know of them?"

"Ach, they're Omanis. It is always about money with them. If you work cheap, they will probably take you. What can your man do?"

"He knows horses," Serafina said, hoping she was not lying. Jalal had said he wanted to work with horses, not that he knew how. Then again, he had not known anything about caravans, either. It seemed he was one who could learn anything he wanted to learn.

"Then, he may get work. Most of our girls they take for cleaners. Look for a big house, they are ones who need them. Not an easy life, but better than here."

"That is what we're hoping." Serafina had no choice but to trust this woman. If she spoke to Bazir, of course, they were done.

"You are young. Once you have a child, try your families again. That usually softens hearts." Dijaya turned to the sideboard where melons were piled in a basket, taking one and whacking it expertly with a cleaver, once through, then once again until she had a wedge. She handed it to Serafina.

"Eat, have a bath and something clean to wear. Simcha!" She summoned one of her children. "Go to Iridis, tell him we need a robe for a boy. Almost grown. Bazir will pay."

"Yes, Ummi," the child said obediently, flying out the door.

Jidaya surveyed her, seeing that Serafina had already eaten the melon down to the rind, then bellowed for another couple of her children circling near the door.

"Bring water for our guest," she instructed. "Put it in the tub, in your room."

"Yes, Ummi," they echoed their brother. Serafina smiled. They were small, but Dijaya had an entire cadre of workers. They might stagger under the weight of water buckets, but they would do exactly as they were told. Domidian children were seldom coddled. Their lives were too hard for that. She was beginning to realize how spoiled she had been.

"You can bathe there," the other woman told her. "I will see you are not disturbed. When Simcha brings a robe, I will hand it in. And don't forget a plate for your man before you go. I am sure it was a hard journey for him, too."

"Very hard," Serafina agreed. "He kept me alive."

Dijaya smiled. "Well, I can see you are a pretty girl. I will give you some oil for your hair, maybe he will like that."

A bath and some of the light amber oil Domidian women used to tame their hair sounded divine. She could not even get a comb through her curly locks without it and she was sure smashing them under a turban for weeks hadn't improved matters.

By the gods, it was good to be a woman again. She wondered if he would care.

CHAPTER 9

Jalal was grateful for the plate she brought him, and happy for her good fortune. Their camels had been turned loose in a yard to eat and drink and rest without their cargo, so he sat with his back to one of the brick walls with the load piled beside him, guarding it.

They slept that night in their respective bedrolls, mere feet apart, but for once she slept soundly, feeling clean and well fed. Bazir was generous with his caravaners, as many bosses were not. But they had come through alive, with their loads intact, and that would save him money in the end.

"Ready for the mines?" he inquired next morning, circling and surveying them along with the others. The men had built a fire and made warm gruel, welcome after the chill of the night. It was something Serafina would never have touched back in the caravanserai. But huddled in the shelter of the oasis, she downed it with gusto.

There was a general groan of agreement. This, after all, was why they had made the trip. If they got it to the border intact, each man would receive substantial payment. Salt was the precious gold of their world and actually worth more. One could not live in a hot climate without it.

That was not why her heart sped up. The mines meant Omana. Soon she would be seeing the border of which she had dreamed. Most likely it would just be more sand, she told herself, but still she could not restrain her excitement. It was sand she had never seen and that made it desirable.

She was still riddled with guilt over the way she had left Ummi, but she told herself that her mother had left her no choice. There was something in her that could never be satisfied with the life her mother and grandmother had led.

"All right, up you get." Jalal broke into her reverie. She had finished her gruel and got to her feet, shaking out her robes. Dijaya's son had purchased not only robes, but the cotton pants men wore beneath them, new boots and also a pair of sandals. Hers were worn out. When she unwrapped the package, she found Dijaya had stuck a small jar of oil and an even smaller one of perfume inside, and Serafina smiled. She would not see the older woman again to thank her, but she was sure Dijaya knew.

This time she walked, guiding the camel on one side while Jalal took the other.

"Miss me?" she teased the big animal. He simply plodded along, head up, occasionally looking around him, and she wondered if he was regretting leaving his hay and water. He could make a bleating sound that reminded her poignantly of a goat and made it then, as if protesting his lot, but then he lowered his head and went on...just as they did.

* * *

THE GREEN of the oasis was a thing of the past. It was gone along with the shade, the water...everything that made life pleasant.

Now, it was just hard. The land was dry and stony, with low foothills of a sickly grayish-tan suggesting they never got water, not even in the rainy season. She did not see a drop the entire time they were there. It was back to wake up, trudge, shelter a little, trudge some more, eat dinner, fall into an exhausted, uncomfortable sleep. She was so miserable that there were times she simply wanted to curl up against Jalal and have him hold her the way he had done in the storm. But, for many reasons she did not.

That was not to say they did not talk. There was little else to do.

"What do you want in Omana?" she asked him one day.

"Work," he said, walking carefully with the camel. Each step had to be taken with caution because the ground was so dry that every rock and pebble rolled underfoot. The camels were more sure-footed than the humans, but even they sometimes stumbled, which would be a real problem once they carried salt. Bazir had explained how the slabs must ride along their sides, covered and strapped. Any fall or any rain could be a disaster, damaging priceless merchandise. This, Serafina thought, was where Jalal would really earn his money. That cargo would be his responsibility. "What about you?"

"That seems reasonable," she replied. "The woman who fed me at the oasis said they take cleaners in the big houses." She was silent a moment, judging how much of her thinking to share with him.

"The biggest house in Omana is the Seat." She named the capitol, the locus of power, home of the Emperator. "Also the biggest stables, I would suppose."

"Also where you can find the Emperator." Jalal laughed gently. "Do you really think you can meet him?"

"Why not?" she responded. "Even Emperators need their rooms cleaned."

"Or their latrines." Jalal's tone was dry and she made a face at him.

"I do not care what I have to do."

He just shook his head. "Dreamer. You are a dreamer. Even if you get a job there, and I would suppose they are hard to come by at the Seat, you will never see anything more than a scrub bucket. You will have knees the size of melons by the time you are seven-and-ten."

"That is next year," she said breezily. "Anything can happen by then. Besides, you should try to get work as a groom. He has very fine horses, they say."

"They still shit. I will be shoveling shit."

"Everything does." She paused. "Except maybe scorpions. I never saw one of those do it. Do you think they do?"

"You never saw a scorpion," he corrected. "You would have been climbing me like a pole if you had."

She cornered her eyes at him.

"We are just partners in this," he said, unmoved. "If you get a better offer, leave me. If I get one, I will leave you."

"You would leave me?"

"Once you are safe." He paused. "You and I do not want the same things."

She digested that in silence.

"In the meantime," he went on, "be very careful at the mines. Many of the men there are prisoners. They are the lowest of the low. Stay close to me or Bazir."

"Whose prisoners?" she wanted to know.

"Ours." He kicked a rock out of her path that would have sent her to the ground. "It is not only the Havacians and Omanis who arrest us. We have our own patrols."

She knew that. They were the ones who would have flogged her if they had caught her wearing men's clothing in the bazaar. She doubted the foreigners would have cared what she wore. Their women were said to be very free.

"I wonder how different it will be," she mused.

"Greatly," he replied. "They do not share our faith. They have no priests or temples as we know them. The women are very licentious, apparently. They say the Emperator's consort is one of the most beautiful women in the world. She paints, and sometimes sits with him in judgment, and gives entertainments for the people."

"She sits with him?" That was a whole new concept. "He must love her very much."

"Apparently." Jalal kicked another rock. "Why don't you keep your eyes on the ground? That is where you have to live, you know—not in your dreams."

"But what is life without dreams?" she asked wistfully.

He had but one word for that. "Longer."

It might be safer, Serafina thought, but there were things other than that. She would like to see a beautiful woman whose husband loved her in that manner.

Jalal was a good man. But he was never going to be an Emperator.

* * *

THE MINES WERE UGLY. Long tracks led into their openings, sunk into low hillsides of brownish-gray soil studded with rocks, stretching to the horizon. The only things above ground were miners' shacks and work pits with some sort of scaffolding, wooden beams that stuck out like scarecrows in a field.

"That is where they cut and load the salt," Jalal told her.

She looked again at the mine entrance. "That looks like a portal to the underworld."

"Pretty much," he agreed. "The work is bad. Hot and dark, and the salt ruins lungs. No one in their right mind would agree to work there. That is why they use prisoners."

The men were ugly, too—many of them wasted wraiths who stared at them with an expression somewhere between dumb hatred and dangerous insolence. Serafina shivered, instinctively edging closer to Jalal.

"Stay with me," he repeated, "or near Bazir or even Hagid. He has been fairly useless as far as I can see, but he is better than nothing."

She bristled slightly at the insult to the boy who had offered friendship. "He is all right. He just misses his family, I think."

"So do I," Jalal said, beginning to remove the load from their camel, as the others were doing. He worked rhythmically, without pause. One load would be replaced by another. "But here we are."

"You miss Imrun?" she asked, incredulous.

"No. Hesta. She will grieve."

There was little she could say to that, thinking of her mother.

"We could send a message from Omana," she suggested. "Imrun has no way to reach us there. Just let them know we are safe."

Jalal made a sound implying Omanis would not give a rat's ass if they cared to send a message, but he didn't comment, busy lifting down the load. Although she was faintly annoyed with him, Serafina made haste to help. Bazir was not paying them to stand around longing for home. He was busy, pacing down the line, encouraging them to pile their cargo. She didn't have to be told they would sleep with it again, guarding it. The men she saw would kill their own mothers for a dinar.

"Water at the well," Bazir called. "Two flakes of hay for each camel. That is all I can get. Tether them for the night, stay with them, and in the morning we will load. You will be brought food to carry. We leave again as quickly as possible."

That suited her. She had no desire to linger at the salt mines of Domidia and did not sleep well that night. She doubted Jalal slept at all, and for the first time he revealed a dagger he had concealed prior to that and slept with it close to hand. At first, she was startled, but most Domidian men carried one, if not in plain sight. Before they were conquered, her country had boasted one of the most skilled leagues of assassins anywhere in the world. Wealthy men hired them to remove political enemies or even just those who had offended them. They had been much in demand.

Seeing it, she slept a little better.

In the morning, as promised, surly workers brought them sacks of beans and dried meat and flour that appeared to be all they would get. She strapped it on the camel's shoulder while Jalal filled water skins that he would hang from the pommel of their saddle. Once that was accomplished, though, he began strapping on evil-looking bands that would secure heavy slabs of salt. For the first time, their camel whirled and tried to bite.

"He recognizes those," Serafina noted, sadly.

"No doubt." Jalal whacked his nose just enough to discourage him, not enough to hurt. It was like hitting a bony rock, anyway—more likely to hurt you than the camel. "But this is his job."

"And ours," she said sourly.

"Well, do you want to get to Omana or not?" He was already tired, Serafina thought, and softened her tone.

"Of course I do. What can I do to help?"

"Hunt as we go," Jalal suggested. "We will be going into better country, apparently, but without much food, and you are getting good with the sling. See what you can find."

It was true. She had shown an affinity for propelling the smooth stones used to bring down small game, and she was quiet and stealthy and did not cavil at the necessity. The girl so reluctant to see animals killed that she had taken leave of Ummi's stall was gone. She was a different person now, or perhaps the one she had always been.

* * *

WITHOUT SORROW, she watched the mines disappear behind them as they urged their heavily laden camels through well-worn paths between the hills. The salt slabs were heavy and cumbersome, covered with hides that slid and had to be constantly readjusted. That was Jalal's job, while hers was to mind the camel, and she was not sorry when he suggested she take a break to hunt. Gratified, she noted that he didn't urge her not to become lost as he had done at the beginning.

City-bred, nevertheless she had quickly developed a sense of direction and a knack for retracing her steps, reading trail marks that she knew she would never have noticed only three months before. Her skin grew parched and cracked from the arid conditions, her clothes were constantly gritty and she was more than grateful for socks Dijaya had purchased for her, because she did not develop blisters as some of the others did. Many of the men were limping and some of the camels, too. They were becoming a tattered band, not the same group that had left Someno.

"Ah, yes, this is the worst part," Bazir commiserated with them one night, sitting at their camp fire because they had offered to share roasted hare with him. She had been successful in her hunting that day, though one hare for three people was hardly luxury. It was more a courtesy than anything else. She had made simple travel bread from flour and water and salt, wrapping it around warmed beans, and that was mainly what they ate.

"You were lucky to find this," Bazir commented, licking

one of the little bones clean. "Even the animals do not like to live here."

"Will we soon be out of it?" Jalal asked.

Their leader nodded. "Only another fortnight here, at most." He sighed. "Then the green hills of Omana."

"Really?" Serafina inquired, afraid that he was being sarcastic, but he nodded.

"Yes. We will cross a river and then the land begins to change. It has water then, you see. The Omanis raise animals there that do not require much pasture—sheep and goats—and then the small farms begin. There is a processing point for our salt and, more importantly, a paymaster."

Jalal laughed. "Most important."

"I think we will do well," Bazir judged. "The salt is of a good quality and has traveled well. There has been no rain that might have spoiled some of it. And this crew has been good." He glanced back at the men gathered by their camp fires. "Some of them I already knew, some I did not and took a chance on them. Like you."

He looked steadily at Jalal. "Have you decided what you will do?"

Serafina held her breath. It was a good offer Bazir was making and Jalal had spoken of leaving her if he got one. She did not want to believe that he would. The thought of it was like thinking of cutting off her leg. But he could. They did not want the same things, he had said. She knew that was his way of saying she did not want him, so he would not consider himself bound to her indefinitely.

But he nodded. "My brother would like to see the wonders of Xanthus."

Bazir just raised his brows. "Xanthus? That is a good far trip."

"I thought perhaps we could ride with one of the wagons

taking the salt," Jalal explained. "In exchange for our work, as we did for you."

"Well, I will give you a good recommendation if that is what you want." Bazir threw the bones into the fire. They did not leave litter behind them as many caravans did. Whatever was left in the morning would be buried, leaving a clean campsite for whoever came next. He was careful of where they dug latrines, too, saying they must not be close. Serafina sensed he was one of the better caravanners and that Jalal had chosen wisely when he picked him out.

"Another two weeks," he repeated, smiling at her. "And you, young man, can see the city. Just be careful not to have your pockets picked there. Have your first woman, but let Jalal choose her. Many are diseased."

Cursing it, Serafina felt herself color to the roots of her hair.

Jalal coughed. "It may be a bit soon for that."

"How old are you?" Bazir inquired kindly.

Serafina could barely speak. "I turned six-and-ten while we were on this trip."

He winked at her. "Old enough. Just listen to your brother."

She thought Jalal might choke and handed him a canteen. "Oh, I will," she assured Bazir. "Every word."

After he had gone, Jalal just silently rolled over, shaking with laughter. "You are an evil little witch, you know," he finally said when he could speak.

"Well, I'm old enough," she replied, insouciant. "Bazir said so himself."

He gave her a penetrating look. "Are you?"

They both hesitated. In Domidia, she was now old enough to marry and begin a family. If women did not start when they could, often they did not live to raise their children. The poor died young and easily.

She wondered if it would be different in Xanthus.

"I am old enough," she repeated. Jalal just looked at her.

"I do not want you out of pity," he finally said.

She met his gaze, unflinching. "It would not be pity. I am not the same girl you knew."

It was true. She had done things...could do things...she had never even contemplated. Her skin was beaten, her eyes lined from the sun, she was lean in a way she never had been, but those were only the physical manifestations. Something else had changed in her, as well. She felt stirrings she had never felt before.

"We will see," Jalal said.

CHAPTER 10

Bazir was right. Within the fortnight, sprigs of green began to appear and little rills of water trickled from clefts between the hills. A few stunted trees were sighted, some with birds roosting in their branches, and Serafina's sling and others brought in some of those plus hares and bushy-tailed desert squirrels. Buoyed by those and, more importantly, by softer ground underfoot, the caravan made good time.

Ahead of her one day, she saw Hagid waving excitedly at something she could not yet see.

"What?" she gestured at him, shading her eyes, but she still couldn't make it out.

"Go ahead," Jalal said, taking the camel's lead rope. "See what it is."

She saw what it was—water, a thin gray line snaking across the horizon.

"Is that a river?" she asked.

He nodded enthusiastically. "Not much of one, but that's good. It will be easy to cross. That is the border with Omana."

Camels and men alike waded gratefully into the shallow waters.

"Is this all?" Serafina asked Bazir, scooping up the precious substance to clean her face. Everyone else was doing the same, and the camels were drinking.

"It is here," he said. "This is the ford. We must cross here where the water will not reach our salt. Other places are too deep."

"Are there fish?" she asked, thinking immediately of her stomach.

"Once we pass," he responded. "We will let the waters settle until they come back and then catch some."

It was exactly what they did, eating fresh fish her body immediately informed her was the best thing it had had in a while. It was necessary to unload and reload the camels, a heavy and arduous business, but Bazir said they needed rest and grass as desperately as the men needed food. Omana could wait another day for them.

Promptly at dawn, they set out again, with greater energy this time.

"Look!" she told Jalal, grabbing his arm in excitement. "It is true. There are farms."

They were poor affairs, but the first she had seen. Houses of clay brick began to dot the landscape along with wooden sheds for animals. To her delight, Serafina saw sheep dogs busily circling flocks with young boys whistling them to their task.

"See how clever they are," she marveled. Domidia was more prone to keeping hounds that could be helpful at hunting, but they were hard to call back.

The camel snuffled behind them as if commenting.

"Perhaps he thinks the sheep are his brothers," she laughed.

Another half day brought them to a small settlement

framed by hills. There was a camel yard, storehouses, loading platforms and a cluster of buildings that reminded Serafina, poignantly, of a small caravanserai. Here the local farmers had brought meats and produce and their wives had woven clothing and blankets welcomed by caravaners whose bodies and possessions were worn out.

The salt was unloaded with great effort, to be pieced and put into the storehouses. Loads that had already been processed waited in a multitude of wagons that would head south, through the length of Omana. Salt was in demand everywhere. They would have no trouble selling the product anywhere it could be unloaded. Shouting men and boys circulated freely and Serafina saw Bazir making his way through them to the paymaster's station. So did Jalal, who lifted down the last of their cargo with token assistance from her and real help from the others. If they wondered why she did not handle the really heavy loads, they didn't comment. She had been a good worker otherwise, handy with the camels and roundly congratulated when she brought game to the campfires.

"Looks like our pay will be coming," he said. "Are you sure you wish to go south?"

She gave him an exasperated look. "I have not come this far to turn back now."

He shrugged. "All right. I am just asking."

Truthfully, she was overwhelmed. She stood on Omani soil, among men who spoke both tongues, differentiated in large part by their dress. Omani men never wore robes, or turbans. Instead, all of them wore tunics and loose pants. Some were bearded, but many were not. And to her great surprise, she saw women by the small group of buildings—gowned, hair uncovered, moving among the men. Such a thing would never have happened in Domidia. It was true, then. The women were free, or nearly so. She found herself staring at them.

Jalal, following her gaze, smiled. "You will not be able to travel as a boy here. Once you take your turban off, there is no disguise."

"It's all right," she said. "I cut off my hair."

He just shook his head. "It will not matter."

"Then I will leave my turban."

"You cannot," he told her. "It is prohibited. Omanis may not kill us now, but they did. Their commanders told them to kill anyone wearing one. They have never entirely forgotten that."

This was something she had never considered.

"It should be safer here," Jalal tried to reassure her. "There are regular patrols on the Omani roads—the Emperator's men, peacekeepers, or so they say. When Bazir pays us, you can buy women's clothing. I will be getting clothes as well. Our robes will mark us as foreigners."

"I cannot cover my head at all?" she asked, aghast.

"I think not." Jalal's voice was firm. "We would stand out and you do not want that."

No, she didn't. But she was going to feel naked. She had expected more freedom in Omana, but not this much.

"Get a gown," he said. "See what the other women wear and buy that."

She hesitated.

"You will look pretty," he encouraged her. "Tell the women you are going to be on the road and they will know what to give you."

She doubted many women took to the roads, but maybe they would help her anyway. This was going to be an experience.

Eventually, after Bazir paid them, she made her way hesitantly to the buildings. The vast majority of customers were men, while the women she had seen mostly stood behind counters, only going outside to replenish their stock. Heart in her throat, she edged up to one of the counters, silently unwinding her turban and removing it while a buxom Omani woman watched her, equally silent.

"I need women's clothing," she said, in Omani.

To her relief, the other woman smiled. "So I see. You traveled as a boy?"

"It was safer."

"No doubt. Well, where do you go now?"

"Xanthus."

The woman raised her brows, but she was already turning to the shelves behind her. "Xanthus? That is brave of you. Do you have companions?"

"Yes." Serafina didn't elaborate.

"You have family there?"

She took a deep breath. "My father is there."

He might not be, of course. He might be a life's journey away, in Havacia, and she could not go that far. If only her mother had been willing to tell her who he was, she thought resentfully, none of this would have been necessary. And though she knew her mother loved her, it must be that she was secretly ashamed of her, or she would have said. She could have given his name, but she never had, and neither had Imrun.

"Ah, I see," the woman said, looking at her more closely. "Havacian?"

There was no disguising her fair skin and green eyes and perhaps it was just as well, now. What had sometimes been a disgrace in Domidia should serve her well in Omana, where many Havacians still remained.

"Yes."

"Well, here is what you will need," the woman said, blunt and practical. Her fingers had already been trailing the shelves as if she needn't even look, and she loaded material in her arms. "Gown, shawl, stockings and shoes. The stockings tie with these, at the top." She handed Serafina two lengths of silk. "It may be a little cold at times and it rains further south. I suggest a cloak. You have boots?"

"Yes," Serafina said quietly. The cloak, at least, had a hood.

"Rags, here is some bath oil, some combs." She smiled at Serafina. "Your hair is very curly. You can use these until it grows in."

She threw in the silver-colored combs. "You speak good Omani. That should help. Stay with your companions and you should have no trouble. They are Domidians?"

"Yes," Serafina said, seeing no need to say there was only one. And she fully intended to stay with him.

"Well, good luck to all of you. Now..." She totaled up the items rapidly. "You have Omani scrip?"

"Yes." Serafina counted it out, familiar with it because Omanis had bought at the caravanserai.

"Good," her momentary friend commented. "You know our money. That will help. Not everyone will be honest with you."

"No, I did not think so," Serafina replied.

"And you are not stupid."

She leveled a look at the other woman. "Does everyone suppose Domidians are?"

"They will try to take advantage of you. Don't let them."

Serafina remembered the dagger Jalal carried. It had surprised her, but then she'd had many surprises along the journey. Somehow, she did not think anyone was going to take advantage of him. She had never seen him be unpleasant with anyone, but now she supposed he could be. A man did not carry a dagger unless he was willing to use it.

"You can change your clothes in the back," the woman

told her, gesturing behind the counter, “now that you have bought them.”

No one was taking advantage of this lady, either.

“Later, I think,” Serafina declined. “If I return, can I still do it?”

“Yes, of course.” The woman smiled at her. “You are not forgettable.”

She stopped only long enough to purchase a bit of food at one of the other counters, where the women selling it gave her a looking over because she was a woman wearing a boy’s robe. But everyone came to their buildings and everyone had a story. In that way, it was just like the caravanserai, just smaller. As long as she had money, no one inquired. Carefully, she rewound her turban before returning to the train.

Jalal looked at her, questioningly.

“I will change when they have gone,” she told him, holding out a small package of Domidian candy she had purchased. Once, it would have been nothing of note. Now, the candy of ground seeds, honey and nuts tasted like Heaven. “I do not want Bazir to know we deceived him.”

“Good thinking,” he said. “They did not overcharge you, I hope.”

“I know at least ten currencies,” she assured him.

He just laughed. “You are your mother’s daughter.”

“Yes,” she said. Imrun could not touch her in Omana and perhaps he had never sought them. There was no way to know. But she missed Ummi. She realized then that she really had not given much thought to what would happen after she reached Xanthus. Could she ever return to Domidia? There were some bridges, once crossed, that you could not cross again.

“I have a ride for us,” Jalal told her. “You will not have to work this time. I paid.”

"Really?" She could hardly believe her good fortune, or his generosity.

"You paid most of our way here," he explained. "It is only fair."

"Thank you." She looked at him critically. It was rare to see Jalal without his turban, although she had. His hair had grown and he had pulled it into a topknot such as some of the Omani men wore, but there was no disguising what he was. His was desert blood, no two ways about it. Considering how much time they had spent there, she considered it fortunate. Whether or not it would be a disadvantage in Omana, she didn't know.

"You look good," she complimented him. Unlike many men in the caravanserai, who had ready access to rich food and indolence, Jalal had never been anything other than fit. Now, honed by hard work and hardship, he looked like the desert riders who had traditionally fought not only other tribes, but the Havacians and Omanis who had invaded Domidia. She hoped it did not work against him.

There was a sound of footsteps behind them and she turned, seeing Hagid approaching.

"You are staying?" he asked Jalal at once. His face fell when Jalal nodded.

"We want to see Xanthus," Serafina explained, feeling guilty. It was not necessary, Jalal had told her, since there was always some exchange of men at the Omani border. Some always wanted to go on, while others would gladly sign on with Bazir to give him a crew returning to Domidia. They would not be missed except by Hagid.

"You might take our camel, if Bazir will let you," she tried to assuage her guilt. "He never spits or bites like the others."

"No, they are going to rest the ones we brought," Hagid told them. He shifted awkwardly foot to foot. "Well, I am sorry to lose you. You were good to travel with."

Jalal smiled at him. "Behave like a man, Hagid. That's all you're lacking. You're a good worker. Just let the others know they can't push you around."

He was a mediocre worker at best, but Serafina knew Jalal was trying to be kind. And Hagid did need to take his advice.

"Goodbye, my friend," she said. "We will remember you."

"Take care." She could sense he was keeping his farewell brief. He was disappointed and didn't want them to see it. Perhaps he was listening to Jalal, at least a little. Turning, he began shuffling back to where fresh camels were loading for the return trip, bearing the spices and silks and other cargo she had watched coming into the caravanserai for years. Never had she suspected what it took to get it there.

"Go change, they're leaving now," Jalal told her. "So will our ride. Unless you want to do it here."

She smirked at him. They were standing in full broad daylight. "So you might wish."

"I might," he said mildly. "But not with an audience. Go and change."

She felt a flush of heat, willing herself not to succumb to one of her dreaded blushes.

I am not a girl any more, she told herself.

Apparently, he had noticed.

CHAPTER 11

The ride Jalal had found for them was simply a cramped space in one of the wagons, covered because it carried supplies to feed this caravan.

"For weeks, we didn't have enough food," she lamented with a smile, "and now it is falling on us."

Jalal looked around before they boarded. It was busy with men hitching teams, loading freight and paying no attention to them.

"Wait a moment," he said, pulling her to the side of the wagon in the shade of a low, spreading tree. Standing close to her, he slid his dagger into her palm, still sheathed.

"Tie to this to your leg, under your skirt, with one of your garters," he said quietly. "I will be searched."

She just sucked in her breath, suddenly afraid.

"They are still wary of our men," he explained. "Not the women. You won't be touched. They think you are harmless."

She bent quickly, using his body and the side of the wagon to obscure vision. "Well, that's a mistake," she muttered, securing the dagger with shaking fingers. Domidian women were obedient to their men, but during the wars noblewomen had padded cut-down chain mail with their silk shifts and fought beside them.

He laughed softly. "If you knife someone, don't go for the heart. Go for the gut. Easier target."

She moved away from him as their driver approached. They were just in time. An Omani guard—one of very few they had seen—came with him.

"Passengers?" he asked, and Jalal nodded. "Turn around."

Jalal's disdain was unmistakable, but he stood quietly for the indignity of being searched, his glance at Serafina telling her to hold her peace. This was the price of crossing the border. Had they returned to Domidia, there would have been nothing further to endure. But if they wanted to traverse Omana, that was another story.

"Where are you bound?" the guard asked, stepping back.

"Xanthus."

He just grunted. "It's a long trip. Get going."

The driver had waited, but now took his seat behind two heavy horses while, to her surprise, Jalal took her hand to help her into the rear of the wagon. Dressed as a boy, she had not been able to receive such courtesies. Now, simply because she wore a gown, she did.

"Sit on one of these," he instructed, tossing in their bedrolls. "Your tender behind is going to suffer this trip."

The guard had left, but the driver guffawed. "He's right, miss. It's a long ride to Xanthus."

* * *

THEY RODE in a line of wagons and flocks of sheep being herded by young boys and sheep dogs—a caravan of a different sort. The driver, happy to chat on what would be a long and hopefully uneventful journey, told them bands of cattle and oxen would join them as they drew closer to the city.

"It takes trains like these going into Xanthus every day to supply it," he explained. "These are the northern caravans. The ones from the south come from Antros, the seaport, and barges come on the river. Xanthus is enormous. Yours is not the only salt, though it's the best. They have drying pits near the sea, at Ilsana, and that comes, too. And of course the Emperator's estate, Cana, sends food, lots of it."

Serafina latched onto that mention of the Emperator, the man on whom her hopes were now pinned.

"Have you ever seen him—the Emperator?"

The driver nodded. "He speaks to the people often—not like the others."

"Do you like him better?"

"I don't remember the others. We were conquered by the Domidians for too long." He glanced at Jalal meaningfully, though not particularly hostile.

"He's given us peace and done well. He was our first foreign Emperator, you know. That is why they call him the Father of Omana. He came to us when we had no one else, but now there is his son." The man nodded as if satisfied. "He is very much Omani, like his mother. He won't be turning foreigner on us."

"What is his name?"

"Dario. Prince Dario, people are calling him." He glanced at her. "He's about your age. His mother is Lady Guilia. Very fine lady. She does a lot of good for the people. And there is a daughter, Lissa. It's a quiet Seat, compared to the others. Not too many scandals."

"We always heard there were, in the old days," Jalal said carefully, keeping his tone neutral.

Their companion shrugged. "That's what I heard, too. Couldn't tell you. I just work with what we've got now."

"A wise policy," Jalal agreed.

"Suits me." The driver pulled up briefly because sheep were crossing their path, this time accompanied by goats that had not been with them at the beginning. Their horses stood patiently while the errant strays gamboled about them for a minute, but panting dogs came up quickly behind them, nipping at their heels so that the goats trotted nimbly off the road, the bells on their collars ringing, while the sheep followed. The driver clucked to his horses, which started up again with a little jolt that sent Serafina back against Jalal. She felt him brace her with his arm as they sat squished in between the driver's seat and his supplies.

"No man loves taxes," their companion went on, "but we 'ad worse, under the Domidians. Money stays the same week to week, no paying one price this week and another the next. The people 'ave work, mostly, an' the city's cleaner than it used to be. H'aint been a war since Domidia and he led troops himself. He's no coward. All in all, he's done a good job."

"Don't you have an Empiricum to regulate those things?" Jalal inquired.

"Aye, but ever'body knows he runs it. They tried to start an insurrection, and he hanged the lot of them. Personally, they say. Got the priests in hand, too—told 'em they'd get the same, did they make trouble."

"Oof," Serafina commented. "You can't do that in Domidia."

"Which is why you got no money in Domidia," the driver pointed out. "They take it all."

Jalal laughed—something he wouldn't have dared at home. Serafina knew he held no high opinion of their priesthood, though he couldn't say much. No one could, for fear of the religious patrols. Now, apparently, he felt safe enough to do it, and enough to do something else, as well. He had never taken his arm from around her and when she felt him nudge her gently, she moved back obligingly against him.

"Don't fall off," he murmured.

She wasn't about to fall off, but his arm around her felt good. Tentatively, she rested her head against his shoulder. It was hard as a rock, but a comfort. She still remembered the way he had held her through the storm. Now, no danger threatened except the one she had felt slowly building inside her for a long time.

They would see, he had said. She just smiled to herself.

THE FURTHER SOUTH THEY TRAVELED, the more verdant the land became. For the first time in her life, Serafina saw fresh water in plenty. It ran in streams and rivulets throughout the countryside, sometimes pooling in places where people had erected little plaster statues of what she supposed were their gods.

Small farms and then bigger estates began to dot the landscape, with many orderly rows of trees lining the roads, which were cobbled and good for the most part. There would be no carts sinking to their hubs in seasonal mud and it was said troops could move along them at great speed.

"What are those?" she asked Jalal, beginning to see upright stone edifices along the road.

But their driver answered. His name was Ricio and he had proven to be a veritable fountain of information. Since all of it was new to them, though, they welcomed it.

"Mile markers," he said. "There's one each mile so you always know where you are and how far it is to where you are going."

"That's helpful," Jalal remarked, and Serafina knew he was remembering the trackless wastes of the desert. Only Bazir had known where they were. If he had perished, their luck would have run out.

"It's many miles yet to Xanthus," Ricio told them. He seemed to welcome them moving to the front of the wagon to talk with him, though space was limited. Serafina's place was practically on Jalal's lap, but she was growing more comfortable there. He never complained, simply holding her loosely at times when the road was bumpy. One time he had put his hand inside her gown, but she had realized he was checking for his dagger and guided him to it, silently, giving him an impish smile. He had stroked her leg briefly, and then had not done it again. She was more shocked by her own reaction: a simultaneous loosening and chill in her body, and the wish that he would do it again. But he didn't. If he was courting her, and she thought he was, he was being very subtle about it.

The long, winding caravan was peaceful and they did see Omani patrols on the road, tough-looking men on good horses who eyeballed them thoroughly, but then nodded pleasantly enough and continued on, picking their way carefully through the sheep and goats and now a few donkeys who followed the wagons. Serafina was never sure where the extra animals came from, but supposed farmers had sent them for sale. It would save them a long trip if they sold them to the caravan, though they would get less money than if they had taken them to the city themselves.

"It's spring," Ricio explained. "They don't want to take time away from planting."

It had taken Serafina almost by surprise to see the trees and bushes leafing out, some of them showing red tips denoting buds. Changes of the seasons were much less noticeable in Domidia. In Omana, the pastures were full with foals and calves, lambs and kids, and baby chicks and ducklings sprinkled farmyards and ponds. Once, a sow ran across the road right in front of them, with black piglets like little dots of ink following her. The men caught fresh fish nearly every night. This was a rich land.

"Aye," Ricio agreed when she commented. "That's why your king—when you had one—was so anxious to take Omana."

"Well, there's no more king," Jalal said shortly. Instead, a ruling partnership of mainly Omanis, and the occasional Havacian, kept their land under occupation.

Ricio shrugged. "Sorry, boy, it's just the truth. Yer King and nobles stole what yer priests didn't, until there was nothing left for the rest of ya, and then they had to go look for it somewhere else."

"You had your own problems." Jalal still wasn't ready to capitulate.

But their driver seemingly never took offense. Jalal helped readily with the horses and distributing food to the other wagons even though he was paying for the privilege of a ride, and Serafina often cooked up something better at night than the other drivers got. She thought Ricio liked them well enough, on the whole.

"Didn't we just!" he laughed. "Whole train of ungodly corrupted men on the Seat, from what I've heard. They sent enough of us off to do their dirty business, fighting wars we didn't even know nuthin' about."

He shook his head. "So many of them boys never came home. We lost 'em in Domidia, we lost 'em in Alcinia—all places we needn't never have been. Emperator Iberis, the last one, was the worst. Broke the treaty with Alcinia, then hired the Tumagis to go in and get their tin for him and all hell broke loose all over the North."

Serafina listened, fascinated.

"We're still payin' for that one."

"How?" she prompted. This had something to do with her father, but she had never known just what.

"It was afore yer time," Ricio explained. "We 'ad a treaty to get tin from Alcinia, Iberis broke it before he was even Emperator and paid their enemies, the Tumagis, to go and get it. So's we wouldn't have to send our boys up to get it, ye see. Biggest mistake he ever made. You rile up Alcinis, it's like kicking a hornet's nest. Crazy bastards, beggin' your pardon."

He smiled at her, apologetically. "They're all crazy. Worship some goddess that says they're coming back in other lives, so they don't care about this one. They'll die to kill ya. They say they'll climb up cliffs with arrows in their teeth, just so's they can shoot ya when they get to the top."

"We had some in Domidia, for a while," Jalal agreed. "They're all insane."

Ricio grunted in agreement. "Iberis sent General Magistri up there to straighten it out, only hear to tell it, he fell in love with an Alcinic princess, took the throne and told Iberis to go to hell."

"He fell in love with the throne," Jalal put in.

"Mebbe. I dunno. But he and Iberis hated each others' guts, that's for sure, an' they both got killed in the end. Some of the General's own troops killed him for treason and Iberis slit his wrists in his bath when you Domidians came over the border. They'd have killed him bad, y'see."

That appeared to be for Serafina's edification.

"Very bad," Jalal agreed.

"Then your king got greedy and went after the whole North and eventually the Havacian king got them pulled together and they all came down here and knocked the snot out of ya."

"I remember," Jalal said tightly. "Just barely."

"Well, an' I'm sorry, boy," Ricio said. "Wasn't nuthin' to do with ye. But seems like it's always the little people that suffer.

The big ones just run right over us lookin' for their gold and glory."

He spit over the side of the wagon. "Hope they don't do it again soon."

It was more than Serafina had ever known and helped to explain how her father had come to Domidia. She lay closeted with Jalal that night, thinking about it. Inside the wagon, there was no sound but rain pelting down on the top while streaks of lightning occasionally turned the sky rosy, silhouetting wagons and herds sheltering against them, deep purple shadows against the light. Not a soul was stirring.

"Is it a storm?" she asked anxiously, remembering the haboob.

He stroked her face soothingly—the first time he had ever done it. Gently, his fingers traced the arch of her brows.

"Just a spring rain. It will pass."

"I never liked storms," she confessed.

"I know. You were always afraid."

"And you always told me it would be all right," she remembered.

"It's all right."

She lay still a moment, digesting that. "Do that again."

"Do what? Tell you everything is all right?"

"No," she said. "Touch my face."

He hesitated for a moment, then repeated the gesture, this time tracing a path from her temple to her jaw, feather-light.

"Are you afraid now?"

It was equally possible that he referred to the storm or the touch. But she knew better.

"No," she whispered.

"Good."

Sighing, she laid her face against his chest. It was how he had held her during the haboob and she wondered if he would do it again. Putting one arm around her, he stroked her back. Gently, he framed the back of her head in his palm. "What about this?"

She could feel his body heat, the strength of his chest, even the crinkle of hair through the thin cloth of his summer tunic.

"No, I'm not afraid," she said, raising her face.

He took her lips with great tenderness, simply kissing and then releasing, then kissing again. Instinctively, she put her palms against his chest, but her fingers curled inward. He felt good, solid and right, not someone she could ever fear, but someone she could want.

"Where is Ricio?" she murmured.

"He said he found a cave for the horses, to keep them dry. I assume he's there. Shall I draw the curtain?"

They had left the back flap open to watch the storm, but now she nodded. She could feel her heart pounding as Jalal crawled over their bedrolls to draw and tie the curtain. They were so shrouded in darkness that she couldn't see him crawl back, but she felt him. Stretching out lengthwise against her, he took her in a full embrace this time, one arm around her hips, pulling her against him so that she could feel his need for her. This time, she felt the answer to it in her body, leaning into him, wanting more.

"Kiss me back," he said. "Like this."

Tracing her lips with his tongue, he insinuated it gently, opening her mouth. Startled, she felt him exploring her in a new way and it was not only the kiss. His hand slipped beneath her gown, caressing the smooth skin of her shoulder. Tantalized by the touch, she didn't move even when he lowered her gown, seeking her breast.

"I want you, Fina," he muttered, face against her throat. His teeth scored the skin gently and she shivered, pulling his head closer. When her back arched reflexively, he caressed her there, and over her buttocks, beneath her gown, nearly between her legs. "Do you like that?"

It felt like liquid fire running through her. To her shock and shame—but also her delight—she wanted him to touch her there, and when he did, her whole body arched in gratification, pressing against his.

"Will you?" he asked.

They might never have another chance. The days were filled with people and chores. She nodded just as his lips found her breast, his hand cupping it as he pulled on one nipple, stroking with his tongue, then rimming the nub gently with his teeth.

Suddenly, she needed no instruction. She grasped the drawstrings of his pants, pushing them down as he raised her skirts. For a moment, he fumbled with his dagger, untying the silk that held it. She didn't see what he did with it, too busy registering the feel of his hand between her thighs, stroking the tender flesh as he turned her beneath him. Instinctively, she parted her legs, letting him do it until she was mindless with need.

He held her in the great possible intimacy and she wanted it—the weight of him, the press of his belly on hers, his hips on hers and the strength of his knees holding her legs spread. It felt right, no matter that she had fought against it. That was then. This was now. She shuddered and moaned softly as she felt him between her legs, easing inside her.

Even so, the pain was so sharp and hot that she cried out despite herself, muffling the noise against his tunic. He had not even taken off all his clothes, nor she hers.

He paused. "I'm sorry. Relax."

Easy for him to say.

"Just a bit more," he whispered, and pushed. She gasped because it was more than a bit. Considerably more. She could feel him in places where she had never felt anything, stretching and filling her. It frightened her, but at the same time, she did not want him to stop. He didn't speak. The only sounds in the wagon were those of her gasps. His rocking thrusts moved her bodily, scraping her back along the floor of the wagon, but she didn't care, wrapping her legs around his waist. Waves of half pleasure, half pain rolled through her, rendering her nearly insensible, transported to another place where nothing counted but the feel of his body on hers, in hers. Finally, she was ready for this.

He was young and urgent and didn't take long. Her body jerked reflexively as he gave a strangled moan and emptied himself into her, his warm seed flooding.

He lay on her then, spent, and she could feel his heart hammering.

"Are you all right?" he finally murmured.

"Yes." She stroked his hair where his head pressed her shoulder, tenderly as a mother. Bracing himself on his hands, he lifted off her and she winced. The women had said the first time was hard, and they had not lied. She felt sore and sticky and used, and yet empty, still craving it.

"It gets better," he whispered, as if he knew.

He moved to the side, one hand on her belly, caressing it as she lay, overwhelmed by what they had done. She could have had this before—as a wife, in a safe home with her mother and friends nearby, surrounded by the familiar caravanserai, with children eventually playing at the door, like every other woman.

Instead, she had given herself to a man she had not wed, in a wagon in the middle of a strange country, chasing a dream she might never catch. Jalal could leave her the next day. She could have a child under a tree in Omana. She could find her father in a month or never. He could be dead, for all she knew, with someone simply assigned to continue sending money. It would have stopped, eventually, and then she would have needed someone like Jalal. There was no getting through life alone, no matter how strong you were.

"Can we do it again?" she asked.

"You want it again?"

"You said it gets better."

He laughed softly. "Let's find out."

Lying beneath him in the dark wagon, now she knew why Ummi had done it. Holding him tightly, hers in a way no one had ever been or would be again, she understood.

CHAPTER 12

The morning dawned, pink and rose, with birds flitting through the trees as if there had never been a storm. It was almost as if the night had never passed between them, but she knew better.

Everything was changed. They had made love three times in the darkness and he had handled her with such tenderness and then such strong, deliberate possession that it took her breath away. In one way, it was as if he was not the man she had known, while in another she realized it was exactly who he had always been and she had not wanted to see it. Now she could not pretend it hadn't happened or that he was other than what he was. Jalal's feelings for her were not those of friendship. She could still feel where his feelings had been. He had been right, though. It had gotten better. Much better.

Ricio returned, leading his two heavy gray workhorses that were dry and ready to harness, unlike the others.

"Ah, I know this place," he said when she commented on it. "There's a cavern behind those hills big enough for several teams. I just took my boys in there and bedded down with them snug as bugs while the rest of you drowned."

"Besides..." He winked at Jalal. "I thought you two could use some time alone."

Serafina had to turn aside to keep her face from betraying her, but Ricio just laughed.

"In Omana, love is sacred," he assured her. "Be young, be happy, have babies. It's what people do."

Jalal was boiling coffee and gruel over a small camp fire, saying nothing. The train would not be leaving early. People were barely moving. It had been a hard night.

Leaving the horses tethered and munching morning feed from nosebags, Ricio hunkered down beside the fire, taking his share.

"We will be there in another week. Are you meeting people?"

"No," Jalal replied, sipping cautiously. "We'll just take our chances."

"Hmm," Ricio commented. "Many do. Well, stick to the better quarters if you can. The slums are no place for a foreigner. Go to the fish stalls or the bakers, or the tavernas if they do not look too rough. Let it be known you are looking for work. The parks are all right to stay in for a time, while the weather is good, but they will kick you out eventually. By then, you should know some people. The bakers especially are good—they can tell you who is looking for drivers or men to unload the wagons. Tell them you came with me. Then they will know that you know what you are doing and they can tell you where to find a room."

Jalal nodded. "What about Serafina?"

Ricio looked at her speculatively. "Someone will take her for a house maid. They will like that she speaks our language. Many of the girls don't."

"It is easier to tell me which garderobes to scrub," she said.

Ricio just laughed. "Get yourself some clothes—not what

a scrub woman would wear. The more you look like a ladies maid, the better chance you have to be one. It's a better life."

She just nodded, grateful for the advice.

"When you have the job for a while, mention where it counts that you know a man who would be a good worker in the stables." He looked at Jalal. "That will be your chance to get off the loading docks."

Again, Jalal nodded, taking in every word. "The Emperator has huge stables, they say."

Ricio nodded. "You aim high, don't you?"

He looked again at Serafina. "You look Havacian. That may get you some preference. He is, mostly."

"I know," she replied.

"It can't hurt to try." His tone implied that he thought there was little hope.

He had underestimated her ambition, Serafina thought. People always did.

* * *

NEVER IN HER life had she expected to see anything like Xanthus. As they drew closer, the roads were clogged with people and animals, carts and litters for the infirm, troops marching to and from the capitol, priests, merchants, Omanis and foreigners, the whole of humanity. She could see gray clapboard houses teetering nearly against each other with lines of laundry flapping in the breeze, buildings of brick and stone, edifices of white marble on the gently curving hills above them, and the blue-grey Omani River threading its way through them like an indolent snake.

"There is where you want to go," Ricio informed them, pointing to patches of green open space by the river. "Parks. There are public baths and toilets, just don't overstay your welcome. The patrols will move you on eventually. Go down into the streets, mingle with the people, ask for work. You may even find men on the corners looking for workers. It is usually short-term, but it's a place to start."

He handed them the bag of food he had given them. Serafina had already smelled that there would be every variety of food sold in the streets, but she wanted to hoard their coins until they had work.

"Where is the Empericum?"

Ricio pointed uphill, to the largest collection of buildings. It was too far to see them in detail.

"The Havacian guard will be near the street, at least part of them. You speak the tongue?"

Serafina shook her head.

"Too bad. Even so, you're a pretty girl, so they may be be friendly. If your heart is set on the Empericum, try your luck with them. Just don't take Jalal with you."

She was stricken, understanding. He looked too Domidian. She would have to cozen a guard or two, if she could, and try to get a job while he worked the docks, using her time off to stay with him in some cheap room. Eventually, if she was liked, someone might be willing to give him a chance, if they could get past his appearance.

"I'm sorry," she said.

He shrugged.

"Just mind your manners, save your coins," Ricio advised. "Many a foreigner has worked their way up in Xanthus. The world comes here."

He and Jalal shook hands in parting and then his wagon disappeared amidst many others, leaving them alone. Serafina watched after it with a lump in her throat, suddenly afraid.

"No backing out now," Jalal said, as if reading her mind.

"Let's find a park, I can pitch a shelter until they run us off. If you go to the Empericum, give me the dagger. You can bet they won't let that anywhere near, woman or no woman."

"Probably," she admitted. "All right, let's go."

It was a long walk to the park Jalal had spotted from the docks, but eventually they were there, crossing the river on a massive bridge crowded with people speaking every tongue, wearing every form of clothing and eating a variety of foods that left the air redolent with the scent of spices. Growing hungry, she ate cheese and olives Ricio had given them and drank from a public fountain where everyone else drank, too.

"Look, it comes from the ground," she said to Jalal. "How do they do that?"

"I have no idea." He held out a wooden cup, taking advantage of it. Occasionally, someone looked at them, but no one spoke or bothered them. It was as if Xanthus was a gigantic beating heart that simply went on in its own rhythm regardless of anyone's activities. Ultimately, they came to the park, where it appeared some others had set up temporary camps as well. Then, it took no time for a patrol to appear.

"Domidian, eh?" a burly Omani trooper commented, quickly running his hands along Jalal's tunic and trousers. Serafina didn't know how he held his peace, but he did, with a warning glance at her. Again, she was not searched. Knowing the Omanis believed Domidian women were all cowed and submissive, she stood, silently. If only they knew her Ummi, she thought.

"We don't see many of you," the guard commented. "Speak Omani?"

"Yes," Jalal said. "My wife, too."

So, now she was his wife? But she realized he was saying it for her protection. She could have to find a cheap ring somewhere in the shops. In the meantime, she twined her hands like a shy little desert wife, laughing inside.

"Looking for work?" the guard went on. Serafina held her breath.

"Yes."

"Ask at the docks. Don't stay here long. We want no permanent encampment here. Obey the laws, work, pay our tax, and you will be fine. Otherwise...well...you understand."

They both understood. Domidians were welcomed for their cheap labor, but nothing else. One step out of line and you were in prison or back across the border, and here it would be prison. It was too far to the border.

"We will not be here long," Jalal said.

"Good." The guard glanced at her again. "War child?"

She fumed, but just said, "Yes."

"Ask at the Seat. Our Emperator tries to help such as you, or at least Lady Guilia does."

That was a courtesy Serafina had never expected, but she smiled and nodded. "I will go, thank you."

"We patrol daily," the guard warned. "Don't be here more than a day or two."

With that, he left them and she could breathe again. Jalal just grunted, turning aside to put in pegs for a simple shelter he would use on the sunny slopes of Omana, as he had in the desert. There, it had saved them from the haboob. Perhaps it could save them again.

* * *

SHE HAD NEVER SEEN anything like the Seat. Surrounded by metal gates, walls of brick and guard patrols, it sat on several acres on the highest hill in Xanthus. Most of the buildings were white marble glowing in the Omani sun and neatly graveled paths ran like veins through the entire complex. She had left Jalal behind after ascertaining that she could find her way back. But once you understood the orderly and methodical layout of the streets, it was easy.

She stood with her nose to the bars like a child looking into a sweets shop. In the distance, she could see horses and people moving between buildings at the usual Omani pace—unhurried, as if they hadn't a care in the world. People in the streets walked the same way, yet at the heart of it Omana was a bustling empire that ruled the southern world, with an unequaled appetite for work and workers.

Once, Domidia had done that. But no more. Their conquerors would not let them.

Again, it was not long before a patrol appeared. These were Havacians—taller and fairer complexioned than Omanis, but they spoke the native language, drifting through the crowd of assembled onlookers with deceptive casualness. She had heard the Emperator kept a Havacian guard, not entirely trusting the Omanis although one captained the guard. Her heart was thundering as they stopped to inspect her.

"Pretty, isn't it?" one of them commented. His tone was friendly, not like the religious patrols in Domidia. Everyone feared those.

"Oh, very pretty," she answered. "I had not seen it before."

"New here, huh? Where are you staying?"

The other guards looked bored. She suspected that was not the case. They were listening to every word.

"At the park," she said. "With my husband." She didn't know how much protection that would be from predatory males, but supposed it couldn't hurt. The guard had not spoken out of turn, but men were men. An unaccompanied woman was vulnerable, especially when she was young.

"He didn't come here with you?"

She shook her head. "He knows you probably would not like him here. He wants no trouble."

"Domidian?" the man asked.

"Yes. We didn't want to frighten anyone."

The guard looked amused now. "Honey, we aren't frightened."

The Havacian appeared over six feet tall, armed and armored, not as he would be going into battle, but equipped, all the same.

"Besides," he said, "you're no Domidian."

"Not all," she said.

"Looking for work?"

"Yes."

"Well..." He looked at the others as if seeing that they concurred. "You can go around back to the kitchen and ask if they can use you. I have to check you first."

Remembering Jalal's advice, she had already left him the dagger.

"No offense intended, now," the guard clarified, turning her by one shoulder, running hands over her in a way that would have gotten him clouted, had she been in Domidia. Remembering that Jalal had twice endured this, she was quiet. She understood the difference between searching and groping. Although she had heard bad things said of Havacians, this one appeared to be a decent man, perhaps even trying to help her.

"All right," he concluded, while she held her breath, hardly believing her luck. Maybe the gods favored this enterprise. The guard nodded to another one inside the gate. "Take her up to the kitchen, will you?"

The one inside was Omani, and commented at once on the fact that she could speak to him.

"Your Omani is good," he complimented her. "So many of

you girls don't understand what we're asking, it's a problem. If you're willing to work, you should be fine."

"I've never done anything else," Serafina said, following him up the long, long path to the Seat. Horses and messengers were at the front, but her companion took her to an enormous door at the back.

"You could drive a wagon in here," she commented, and he laughed.

"Don't think nobody tried that yet. Come on, I'll take you to Gisela. She's the housekeeper." He scratched his beard. "Hope you don't like to sleep. She don't."

Regretting that she hadn't had time yet to buy better clothes, Serafina waited nervously with the man, who now looked bored, shifting foot to foot as if anxious to be rid of her. Still, he would not dare to leave her alone in the Seat.

"Is the Emperator in residence?" she asked, hoping it sounded casual.

"He is right now, yes," the guard replied. "Why do you ask?"

"Just wondering," she said. "I have never seen him."

"You probably won't now, either."

"No, of course not," she said hastily. One step at a time, she told herself.

Gisela was a thin, middle-aged woman who reminded her of a mouse, eyes always roving as if suspecting an errant dust mite somewhere.

"You can go," she dismissed the guard, who left without a word.

"So." She made a circle around Serafina, like inspecting a horse for sale. "What have you done?"

"Anything," Serafina said, trying to sound confident. "I worked in a caravanserai in Domidia, now my husband and I have walked and ridden here for several months."

Gisela gave the ghost of a smile. "How many pairs of shoes did you wear out?"

"Several," Serafina answered. "Boots, too. We lived through a haboob, then we rode the length of Omana in a supply wagon. I tended the animals, cooked for the men, whatever I had to do."

"Well, if you survived that, you will do," the housekeeper decided. "Have you found living quarters?"

"Not yet."

"Tell your husband to go to the river bank where the flower sellers are. They know everything. Come back here as soon as you are settled. Shall we say three days?"

"Oh, yes." Serafina breathed out again. "Thank you."

"Don't thank me yet. You have not seen the size of this place. When you get pregnant, by the way, tell me. I will give you lighter duty then. We don't kick our girls out. Lady Guilia will not permit it."

She called down the hallway to yet another guard. They were everywhere, Serafina thought. Was this what it took to be an Emperator?

"See this girl out. What is your name?"

"Serafina."

"What?"

"Serafina," she repeated. It was hardly an unusual name.

"From Domidia?"

"Yes. Someno. It's a seaport."

"I know what it is." Serafina held her breath, wondering if this had somehow jeopardized her employment, but in a moment whatever had passed in the older woman's face was gone.

"Very well," Gisela dismissed her. "Return on Fourth Day. Ask for me. You begin then."

Without another word, she turned and walked away while

the guard loomed up beside Serafina. He was an older man, seeming somehow more kindly and less of a threat. That was probably an illusion, though. If he was trusted to guard the Emperator and his family, it was likely he was a seasoned warrior. She remembered Ricio saying the Emperatis had already tried to kill him once. Rulers led dangerous lives.

"Come along, dear," he said. "I'll show you the way out."

CHAPTER 13

She made her way back through the teeming crowds to where she remembered Jalal had put up their shelter, thinking she would have been unnerved by the press of people if she had not grown up in the caravanserai. It was a relief to find even a small patch of grass where he had provided shade and water. He just looked up inquiringly at her approach.

"I start in three days," she said, seating herself beside him where he sat with his arms around his knees, watching the crowd. The babble of tongues around them was astounding. Apparently, half the world came to Xanthus looking for their future.

"You have the luck of the devil," he said. "Now..." He stood up. "Let me see if I have any. I don't think it's a good idea if we leave the shelter at the same time."

She nodded. "One of the guards said go to the river and ask the flower sellers. He said they know everything."

"Better there than the tavernas," he commented, hitching his tunic and striding down the slope to the river.

Alone, she strung a few wildflowers that had escaped the

crush, making a bracelet for herself. When he returned, she decided, she would chance the public baths. They were free, apparently, and though she shrank from the idea of being naked in a public venue, it was obvious the Omanis didn't care. They were going there in great numbers, laughing and chatting, disappearing inside the columns and not re-emerging any time soon. She had seen women she suspected were prostitutes lounging in shadowed doorways, some of them entertaining men. At least Domidians had the decency to seek shelter, she thought, and then remembered bedding Jalal in a wagon with only a thin curtain for cover.

She might make a good Omani after all.

It was late afternoon before he returned, bearing a paper cone of flowers for her.

"I gave them business." He smiled, handing them down to her. "These won't keep long, but there's plenty of water."

"Thank you," she said, startled. "Did it help?"

"I think so. I am going to the warehouses in the morning. They say they are looking for men and there are rooms to rent. Not very nice, I'm sure, but I can look."

No, she couldn't imagine anything in a grimy warehouse district beset by noises day and night being nice, but they couldn't afford nice. She had not inquired how much she would be paid; one never did. If you were a foreigner, you took whatever they gave you and were grateful.

"I am going to the baths," she decided. "I will find water for these."

They were primroses, inexpensive but bright and cheery. "You can go after me."

"All right," he agreed.

No one troubled her as she entered timidly, borne along by a press of women and girls. Men apparently used one on the other side of the long building that housed public baths and toilets. They were utilitarian, but relatively clean, with numerous attendants to take and hold the women's clothing for a small coin, and Serafina used them, blanching at the necessity but going down into the water with the small vial of oil from the oasis.

Two naked, unconcerned girls smiled at her, speaking to her in a language she didn't understand, so that all she could do was smile back and shrug.

"You speak Omani?" One of them switched.

She was relieved. "Yes."

"You are new?"

"Yes."

Both girls were heavily made up, their eyes outlined with kohl, their hair shiny with oil they were careful not to wash out. The one speaking to her bore tattoos in blue ink that Serafina viewed, fascinated. Roses bloomed and serpents twined up her arms. Domidian women did not wear them. It was forbidden, considered an insult to the God who made them. Apparently, whatever God this girl worshipped was not offended.

"I am Rutka," she said. "This is my friend Laisa. You wish to make money?"

"I have a job," Serafina replied.

"Ooh, la," Rutka said, smiling to take any sting from her expression. "Well, if you want more, the mistress of our house pays well."

"What kind of house?" she asked suspiciously.

Rutka winked at her. "You know what kind. You have pretty eyes. Men will pay for those."

"I am married," Serafina lied.

The other girl was sublimely unconcerned. "Your husband likes money, yes? You will make more in a night than you make in a month anywhere else."

"He will not let me." Serafina oiled herself vigorously, feeling it wise to cut this conversation short.

"Well, if you change his mind tonight, come to our house beside the Temple of Memory."

There was a brothel beside a temple? Well, this was Omana.

"Tell them I sent you," Rutka went on. "I will get a cut."

This girl should have married Imrun, she thought. They were two of a kind. As to changing Jalal's mind about anything, she already knew that was a dream. In him, she had met an immovable object.

"Thank you," she said, rinsing her hair quickly. She had wanted a more leisurely bath, but it seemed that idea could prove unwise.

The other girl, Laisa, had remained mute, perhaps unable to speak Omani, but finally she smiled at Serafina, revealing a startling gold tooth. It took a lot of money to get one of those. She was no beauty, but her breasts were the size of melons, and Serafina supposed that would suffice for many men. Probably Laisa did a brisk business despite her face.

Coupling with Jalal in a wagon was cleaner, she decided. More decent. She wouldn't be ashamed of that. He was one man and she had never been with another one. She didn't think she would want to be. She didn't delude herself that she was in love, but she certainly felt something sweet for him, and she would not betray him. Also, she admitted to herself guiltily, she needed him. No one had to tell her that this place was unsafe for a woman alone. Domidian men were known to be knife fighters, no matter how many times the guards might disarm them, and touchy and possessive where their women were concerned. That reputation was a protection for her.

Dipping a small beaker she had carried to get water for her flowers, she went up the steps from the pool to find the girl who had her clothes.

* * *

THE MAKESHIFT CAMP in the park never really settled for the night, with crying children and wandering dogs disturbing the peace so that she slept fitfully. Her only comfort was Jalal slumbering against her, seemingly undisturbed by the noise. Shortly before dawn, exhausted, she finally slept in his arms.

The sun was up by the time she wakened, eyes gritty and head aching. He was there, dressed and tending a tiny fire he had started to heat water. It would not suffice for anything else, but she dipped a rag, sponging her face and beneath her arms, then rinsing her mouth with what was left.

He handed her dried fish and bread. "I will go today to find work and somewhere to live. Stay until I return. Then if you wish to purchase some clothing, I will stay with the shelter. Bring back a little food. All right?"

"It sounds like a good plan," she agreed. Not being able to go anywhere together was annoying, but if they lost their spot in the park it would be hard to get another, and if they lost their shelter, they would be without any. It was a good one and would be stolen the moment they left it. The other people they saw, though casually friendly, were as destitute as they were or more so. She at least still had a few coins. Many had nothing at all.

"Eh," the man at the next shelter called. "See those buildings?" He gestured down the hill to a couple of square red brick edifices. "Free food there. Medicine, too, for the sick."

"Really?"

Their self-appointed friend nodded. "The Temple feeds people, at least for a while. Then the guard kicks you out, then they feed the next ones who come."

"Well, I'm taking it," she decided, but she looked at Jalal. "Can I?"

"Suit yourself," he said.

She joined a short line of people going downhill. Most had already gone, apparently, but Jalal had let her sleep. Amazed, she saw women in plain gowns handing out cooked chicken and cups of tea. Her stomach rumbled in expectation of something approaching an actual meal.

"Here you are," one said kindly, handing her a skewer laced with chicken, and welcome tea.

"Can I take some for my husband?" she asked timidly. "He had to stay with our shelter." The lie was beginning to come easily.

The older woman nodded her understanding. "Of course. You are Domidian?"

Finally, someone had taken her for what she was...at least, mostly. "Yes."

"Hard for you to get work sometimes, I know. If you have too much trouble, come to the Temple and we will feed you."

"Why?" Serafina asked. "We do not share your faith."

"You may," the serving woman replied, "someday, if you are here long enough. It is not a sin to feed people."

"Thank you," Serafina replied. Did these people seek converts? Well, she would never take their faith, but she would take their food. Jalal had to eat, too, and she took it back to him.

"Umm, yes, they do," he confirmed her suspicion. "Lots of gods. None of them are for us."

"No," Serafina agreed, definite. "The gods of Omana are corrupt and licentious. Everyone knows that."

He just looked at her over his chicken. "Said by the woman who sleeps with me unmarried."

She flushed. "You did not say you required that."

"I don't," he said, and stood up. "I am going to find a job. I'll return by afternoon. If I find a room, I am going to rent it." He had taken her money, of course.

Well, that was quite cut and dried, she thought. He would not marry her, he would select their living quarters and pay for them with her money, and if she didn't like it, he didn't care.

Perhaps she shouldn't have slept with him, she thought. But she knew the minute he had found a place to do it, she would. He might be troublesome in daylight, but in the dark, he treated her like a queen.

* * *

THE DWELLING he found was as bad as she had feared, a third story tenement apartment facing an alley where teamsters loaded drays with wine barrels behind horses that reminded her of Ricio's. Jalal was happy because he had been hired not to load the barrels, but to care for the horses that pulled them.

The apartment was fairly dreadful, two rooms and a shared latrine and water pump in a courtyard, with a rickety bed, furniture worse than second-hand and its share of roaches. Her skin crawled at the sight.

"We will get something better," Jalal assured her. "For now, it is close to my work."

"Yes, the horses practically sleep up here," she replied. "When do you start?"

"Tomorrow. Early."

She stripped the covers from the bed, raising a cloud of dust. "These need washing." She had seen a washtub in the courtyard. "Spread our bedrolls. They will be cleaner."

Though they had been on the grass, they were. She had procured more chicken before they left the park and put it on the wooden table that rocked, with one leg shorter than the other three.

"Good." Jalal reached beneath his baggy tunic. Expecting

to see a dagger, she was surprised when he drew out a small container of wine.

"Courtesy of the man who hired me," he explained. "This is what they haul."

Two wooden cups rode among their few possessions and Serafina put them down carefully, bracing the table while Jalal poured. He pulled out a bench, sitting beside her with his foot beneath the short leg, stabilizing it.

"*Salute.*" It was the traditional Omani toast.

"To our new life," she said, somewhat sourly, and drank.

After two cups of wine, life and even the apartment looked somehow better, the chicken was good, and when Jalal lifted her, kicking and laughing, she clung to him long enough to get to the bed. He knelt over her, stroking her slowly, building her desire.

"Such a pretty thing you are," he said quietly, running the back of his hand over her breast so that she just sighed. "Do you still want me?"

"More than ever," she replied honestly. He stood long enough to strip off his clothes while she squirmed out of her gown, turning to drape it over the bedpost because the thought of it on the floor turned her stomach. Bare-naked together at last, they reveled in the new freedom, kissing, touching, playing, courting each other with increasing purpose until he made love to her vigorously, no longer afraid of hurting her. Their bed rocked noisily, undoubtedly giving great amusement to the tenants below, but neither of them cared, loving at length again and again in their squalid apartment while the Omani sun set.

By the time the moon rose, they were exhausted and unable to do it again. Finally, they lay together in companionship, face to face, caressing each other.

"I had a good offer of prostitution today," she told him.

"What?"

"In the bathhouse," she elaborated. "Two cheap girls from some whore house next to the Temple. They wondered if you would loan me out for a night."

"No," he said, sounding less amused than she had hoped.

"That's what I told them." She ran her fingers gently down the side of his throat and along his collarbone, reassuring him. "I want no one but you."

"And I only want you."

"You have had other women, though, haven't you?" she asked. "You knew what to do."

"I will not say I never had a woman, no," he replied, brushing her belly with his fingers. "But I knew once I had a wife, I would have no others. We are meant for this, the two of us, don't you think?"

"Do you mean you want to marry?" she asked. "I thought you said you didn't require that."

"I don't," he replied. "I only prefer it."

She sighed, unable to formulate an answer.

"Why do you fight me on it?" He sounded genuinely puzzled. "We are here now, you have what you wanted, why not do it? They have magistrates here. It would be accepted."

"I already tell people we are married," she replied. "Is that not enough?"

"But we are not," he pointed out. "It is dishonorable."

"Ah, you know," she half apologized. "I told you, it was never you I was refusing. It was Imrun. And Ummi. I felt like she should have stood up for me and she wouldn't. She had no spine."

"It is because she knew I loved you," he said. "She knew I would always care for you, no matter what Imrun said or did."

"You love me?"

"Always," he replied. "Why do you think I let you catch me?"

She giggled, remembering. Somehow, she had always known where he was, even when she blindfolded herself. Maybe she should have listened to her childish intuition.

"Besides," he said, "you have spine enough for two."

Serafina laughed ruefully. "I tell my mother she bedded a soldier and look what it got her."

"Well, you get it from somewhere," he admitted. "I have never known a woman like you, Fina."

"You never will again," she said confidently. "You work tomorrow, the next day I will go. I don't know when they will let me come back."

"I will give you the extra key, " he replied. "Just come when you can and I will do the same. Make what money you can. The more we make, the sooner we get out of here. I have known worse, but for you I will get something better."

"I believe you," she said. Suddenly, now, she did. She had seen things in Jalal during their journey she had not expected to find—his dogged determination, his level head, and a damned fine body. She loved the feel of him inside her, beginning to get a real and intense pleasure from their joining. She wanted more of it.

But he wanted more of her, too. She didn't know why she couldn't give it.

She had come to Omana with a purpose, she reminded herself. Somehow, one day, she must be able to speak to the Emperator, if only to ask whether he knew who sent money to a woman in Someno because she had slept with a noble Havacian and borne him a baby daughter.

Even if he hung her by the heels for her presumption, she would ask.

"Most likely your father is dead or in Havacia," Jalal said, touching her bare shoulder. "And I am not getting on a ship to try to find him there. That is too far."

"They ship wine to Havacia, do they not?" she asked.

He snorted laughter. "You would stow away on an Omani ship? Are you out of your mind?"

"Probably."

"Undoubtedly." His tone darkened. "Do not even think it, Serafina. That is so dangerous you can't imagine it."

"Oh, I know," she agreed, humoring him. "If I cannot learn anything in Xanthus, at least I have seen it. I do not think I would want to see the North. They say it snows there most of the year and the people are savages."

"Would you return to Domidia?" he asked.

She paused. "I don't know. I should try to let Ummi know I am here, though."

"I already did," Jalal said.

"What?"

"I sent a note with Bazir. He was returning to Someno and he promised to try to get it to her. Nothing fancy, just saying we were in Omana and safe."

Serafina swallowed past the lump in her throat. "I did not know you would do that."

"She is still your mother, Fina," he said quietly. "Simply because Imrun is the way he is does not mean you cannot love her."

"Of course I love her!"

"Well, then, hopefully I have eased her mind. Now, can we talk about something else, since you don't want to discuss what I want?"

She ran her hands down his chest. He was warm and solid, she could feel his ribs beneath the skin, the points of his hipbones, the flat power of his belly. Gently, she cupped him in her hand, playing with him, and he grunted. He was not playing, she realized, feeling him stiffen.

"Are there other ways to do it?" she asked.

"Have you been talking with your girlfriends?"

"Well..." She ran one fingernail gently along the underside

of his penis until he flinched, so aroused that it hurt him. "We do talk. After it happens. First, no one will tell you anything because it hasn't happened yet. Then, after you do it, no one talks of anything else."

"And what did they tell you?" he teased.

"Not what you would be like," she whispered. Their faces were inches apart and she looked into his eyes as if she could see his soul. "I didn't know."

He just smiled. "You still don't."

CHAPTER 14

He left early and she spent the day turning their apartment inside out. If the Emperator wanted a scrubwoman, she thought grimly, he already had one. She scrubbed their quarters from top to bottom, washed everything that didn't move and even put their dying flowers in the middle of the poor table. Roaches would continue to crawl through from their neighbors, but they would get no welcome from her. She crunched every one she found, without remorse, until there were no more.

He still had not returned by afternoon, which she took as a good sign, so she asked one of the other women in the complex where to buy some decent clothes. Then she threaded her way among the alleys and cheap shops to ones that were better, remembering to pause first at one of the dingy ones to find a plain silver band for her ring finger. She already felt married, and it would prevent at least some unwanted advances and look better to the housekeeper. She did not take that woman for a fool.

She only wondered why her name had seemed to give Gisela pause, but then she shrugged mentally. Maybe she had known someone with that name. It could be either Domidian or Omani, so that was likely enough.

Shortly before sunset, Jalal returned. She heard the turn of his key in the lock and looked up, watching him come through. He carried a welcome packet of cheese and sausage and a loaf of the long, crusty bread Omanis favored. She didn't, missing bakoosh, but it was good. And apparently wine was a benefit of his job. He had more.

"Here." He put it on the table, which she had leveled with a brick from the courtyard. "This place looks better."

He didn't, covered with sweat and straw dust. He had taken off his boots, which she didn't have to ask to know they'd be covered in manure.

"They kept you in the stables, I see," she commented.

"That was our agreement." He threw himself in a chair as if too tired to stand and she believed it. And Jalal was used to hard work. If he was tired, it didn't bode well for his new employment.

"And used you like a Domidian," she said bitterly.

"That's what I am." He pulled out his dagger, slicing the sausage. "Sit."

She sat, and ate, and made small talk and, as soon as they had finished, got up and picked up the bucket they had found in the apartment.

"Where are you going?" he asked.

"To get you water. You need a bath."

A bath wasn't really possible, no one could bathe in quarters like theirs, but she lugged the bucket back upstairs, finding him already lying in bed.

He wasn't asleep, though.

"Here," she said, beginning to unlace his tunic. "I will wash you."

"You what?"

"I'll wash you," she said, pulling it off him. "You've been working all day."

"So have you, by the look of things," he said, but he didn't protest further. His boots were already gone, so she just peeled off his socks, then his pants, then his loincloth. He lay naked and slit-eyed on the bed, half asleep but watching while she rinsed out a rag and began to sponge him with the same slow, sweeping motions she had used to soothe Jadda. For a brief, intensely painful moment, it reminded her of her grandmother...of the caravanserai...of Ummi.

Shrugging it off, she smiled down at him, sponging him tenderly. This would be every day now, sweating in summer, drowning in winter, shoveling shit and currying horsehair all over himself, hauling feed and straw, hitching and unhitching teams of huge horses that could crush him without a thought. The men worked as hard as the horses. Wine was a big business.

"Sit up," she said at one point and started on his back, sorry for his fatigue but relishing the feel of his bone and muscle beneath her hands. She enjoyed touching him, treasuring what they found together in the nights, wondering why she had ever resisted it. There would be none of that tonight, though. He was half asleep sitting up.

"I hope my job is easier," she murmured, "though I doubt it."

"If not," he said, "I'll be pleased to wash every inch of you."

She laughed. "No doubt."

Finished, she knelt behind him on the bed, simply putting her arms around him, face on his shoulder, giving comfort.

"Go to sleep now," she whispered. "We can talk tomorrow."

He stretched out with a sound of relief on the sheets she had washed and changed, squeezing her hand, but he was asleep in moments and she detached her fingers, smiling at him unseen. She would always remember this—Jalal working to the bone their second day in Omana to give her a better life.

They were poor people. They had always been poor. A stall in a caravanserai was Heaven compared to what most people had, but they were still poor compared to the way many Omanis lived. She wanted to be one of those people. She would be, one day.

* * *

BRIGHT AND EARLY ON THURSDAY, she locked up their apartment behind her although she couldn't imagine what anyone would steal, since they had nothing, and went to the Seat.

The guard at the front gate just nodded when she said Gisela was expecting her. She thought it was probably routine. Other girls were passing through, too, one at a time, looking at her sideways. She smiled at the nearest one.

"New?" the girl asked. She was clearly a Northern Omani, fair and red haired. They were very unusual in Xanthus and, like anything unusual, probably had value. She was beautiful. Many of the girls were. She would have to be careful of her appearance here.

"Yes, I am Serafina," she said, very civilly.

"Patria," the redhead replied. "You will start in the kitchen, then, I expect." She looked critically at Serafina's clothes—not the attire of a scrubwoman although in no way ostentatious. "You do not look like a house maid, somehow."

"I will do whatever they want," Serafina replied, but her dress already announced that she probably wouldn't. Patria smiled at her as if appreciating her boldness.

"I started there myself," she announced. "Now I care for the children."

"The Emperator's?" Serafina asked.

"Oh, the gods, no!" Patria laughed. "They need nothing from me. No, many of our girls have children and they go to a sunroom where we care for them until their mothers leave at night."

Suddenly, Serafina remembered Gisela telling her to let them know if she was expecting because they did not kick their girls out. Apparently they did not reject their children, either.

"It's a real bonus," Patria said. "They are well fed and taught. Girls fight for the chance to work here. How did you get your job?"

"Because I look Havacian, apparently," Serafina said.

"Are you?"

"Half." She laughed. "The half that shows, I am guessing."

Patria looked at her shrewdly. Well, Serafina would never lie about what she was. Truth always came out and then it was worse. This girl already knew she was a war child. Yet it was said they were well treated, at least in the Seat.

"Those soldiers left many of you," Patria said, but not scathingly. "It is said the Emperator was not pleased. And Lady Guilia definitely was not." She looked into the distance for a moment.

"Well, she has her reasons. It works well for the girls here."

"She is a good mistress?" Serafina asked hopefully.

"The best."

They had reached the kitchens and most of the girls split up to go to their respective stations, Patria among them. Gisela standing in the doorway was a strong incentive for most of them to stop chattering and disperse, but Serafina had nowhere to go, unless she stayed where she entered.

The older woman spotted her immediately, saying something inconsequential to one of the other girls, but walking over to Serafina, looking at her from head to foot.

"Well, the worst you will do to your new gown here is get food on it, and you can wear an apron," she said. "You will stay here. If you cooked for a caravan, you can cook for a Seat."

"Yes, Ma'am," Serafina said, charmingly obedient. Of course, she had gotten what she wanted.

"You can start with chopping vegetables. Domidians are good with knives. Estella?"

A buxom woman who looked like the definition of a cook came over, also checking out Serafina's dress. This one seemed amused, though.

"Chopping for her." Without another word, Gisela turned on her heel. Serafina couldn't tell if she had made an enemy or if the sharp-faced housekeeper was simply that way.

"Come along," Estella said. "We will get you set up."

* * *

OMANIS WORKED every day of the week but the last and practically rebelled if required to serve on that one because it was a day reserved for family. From top to bottom, the society revolved around the family and they gathered then. For Serafina, it signified only that she had a day off and that she had been paid on the previous one.

"Look," she told Jalal, sitting on the bed with him and counting out coin. He also had the day free and also had been paid, but Serafina had been paid nearly double what he had.

He whistled. "Pays to work for an Emperator. Well done."

"I never asked," she said, amazed. "I didn't know."

He smiled at her. "Never trouble good fortune. Well, we can use a walk in a park—not the one we stayed in—and then tomorrow one of us can buy food." He had kept them going with the coins he had held in reserve, but now they could actually afford to eat. If this kept up, Serafina calculated quickly, they could probably leave their less than charming abode in mere weeks.

"Let's look for another place while we're out," she suggested. "Not to rent, just to get ideas."

"You already have ideas," he said.

He was more right than he knew. She had been a sponge during that week, listening to everything said to or around her. And those girls talked a lot. The kitchen was a hub of activity.

"I didn't get out of the kitchen much," she told him, "but that place is huge. Unbelievable. I got lost just looking for the garderobe and they have them even for the servants. There's a play room and school room for the babies and children the girls have and they say they give those who are pregnant light work and a bonus when they have their babies."

"Well, that's lucky," he said.

He was right. It seemed that every time they had the energy for it they ended up in bed and Jalal was not the man to abstain or pull out. He worked hard and took his reward in bed, with her enthusiastic cooperation. She was quite likely to conceive; she was only surprised it hadn't happened yet. The thought did not exactly thrill her, but if it happened, it happened. They would manage somehow. Other people did.

"You know I love it," she said quietly.

"And I love that you love it," he replied, pulling her close for a moment. "Let's walk before we think of something else."

"You never think of anything else," she responded, but she grabbed her shawl. "Let's go."

The day was fair, the crowds happy, and they were both growing more accustomed to the sight of frequent patrols and less apprehensive about them. Many times the guards were helpful, directing people who were lost, retrieving wandering children or inspecting the oil lamps that were sometimes prone to fires. With so many wooden buildings in the city, fire was a real danger and they were extremely alert, especially at night when the lights were lit.

"Do you suppose that's why there are so many guards?" she asked Jalal, wandering arm in arm with him, but he shook his head.

"No, I think there are so many guards because these people blow like the wind and even a popular Emperator can never be sure they will stay under control. They tried to kill him and his family not so many years ago."

"I thought that was the Emperatis," she objected.

"Those old men dirty their hands?" he replied. "Never. They hired cutpurses, told the people their religion was going to be banned and set them on the Seat. They broke in and nearly took Lady Guilia and her son. It was while he was in Domidia. The last time, that is."

His tone was dry. He had no sympathy for the Havacians and Omanis who had left him and so many others orphaned, twice. If he could use them to make money, fine. But he would never love them.

"Is that when he hanged them?"

Jalal nodded.

"I guess I would have, too," she said thoughtfully. "You know what our patrols would have done to people like that."

"Worse," he agreed. "But Domidians don't rebel. That is what made us so strong. Omana has torn itself apart twice. I wouldn't be surprised if they do it again."

She knew Jalal studied these matters much more than she did, and she shivered.

"I hope not. All I want is peace and a home."

He cocked an eyebrow at her. "That's all? Really?"

"Well, and to find who my father is," she admitted. "But it may take a long time. I have not even seen the Emperator."

"And when you do, he will kick you out on your rear," Jalal predicted. "And there will go any hope of peace and a home. Grow up, Serafina. This is a dangerous dream you have."

She didn't answer and he sighed. "Well, let's not look at anything to rent, then. You won't keep your job."

"I will be careful," she insisted.

"Harassing a Noble who doesn't want the world to know you exist? You will be lucky not to end up in prison, and I am not going with you."

She felt like he had punched her.

"You knew why I was coming," she said, flatly.

"Yes, and I thought you would see it was insane and give it up. I see now that I was wrong. Just remember what I said. I will not try to save you from yourself this time."

It was no longer a good day.

CHAPTER 15

Neither of them mentioned it again, but sensing his loss of support, Serafina began to put her energy towards her job. The cook was fairly easy to please, but Gisela was something else. She seemed to take special delight in keeping Serafina running like a jack rabbit, never allowing her to complete one task before demanding that she hurry up and finish another. It was exhausting and she could not help wondering why the housekeeper seemed to have it in for her. Things appeared to have been going well until she gave her name and said where she was from. From that moment on, she could feel a chill in the air, without knowing why.

Estella could not enlighten her, when she asked. "Oh, she's just cranky," she said. "She's always been that way."

There was only one time that Gisela thawed. One morning, Serafina was surprised to see a boy about her own age saunter into the kitchen, sneaking up behind the housekeeper and snaking his arms around her waist. Was it possible she had a son?

"Ooh, you," the woman half protested, turning with a laugh. "What is it you're after this time?"

"Honeycakes," he said, succinctly. "I heard you were baking them today."

"And so we are," she said, laughing again. "Come along, beast, and I will give you some."

Serafina watched in astonishment as the skinny housekeeper and robust-looking boy went back towards the baking ovens. He was handsome, with wavy black hair and just the shadow of a beard.

Estella was chuckling.

"Who is that?" Serafina asked, mystified.

"That is our Prince."

You could have knocked her over with a feather. "Dario?"

"Yes, that is the Emperator's son." Estella laughed at her expression. "Gisela sat with Lady Guilia the night of her labor, they say, and has been close with her ever since. She and the others helped Lady Guilia. It was hard for her because the Emperator was away at the time and could not return in time for the birth."

"That must have been hard," Serafina sympathized, understanding now. "So he comes here to tease her for food?"

"Once in a while," Estella confirmed. "She is like a grandmother for him, I think. One of his is dead and the other is in Havacia."

"That's a long trip." Serafina remembered Jalal's comment afresh. He was not going there with her, he had said, nor to prison either.

Well, she had no intention of going to prison. And she had no intention of staying in that kitchen.

She had pursued a friendship with Patria, one that they could exercise only when one of them was free and that was more likely to be Patria. Not long after that morning, she saw her friend lounging near the kitchen and edged up to her cautiously, watching for Gisela. She would break up any conversation she saw forming among any of the girls, but especially Serafina.

Psst," the other girl said quietly. "Do you want to do something besides chop?"

"Definitely," Serafina muttered. There had to be something else to do in a place as vast as the Seat. She thought she would gladly scrub garderobes rather than tolerate Gisela much longer.

"They are going to need another girl in the play room. Do you like children?"

"Oh, I love them!" Serafina lied. She was not drawn to them the way so many women were, but if they were the means to escape the kitchen, she could love them.

"I will put in a word for you," Patria said. "I think you are wasted in here."

Serafina wondered what she would owe for this kindness, but that would probably only be revealed in time.

"It's much more interesting there," Patria added. "Sometimes Lady Guilia even comes in, and her daughter."

That clinched it. She didn't care what she would owe Patria. Getting near to the Lady could mean getting nearer the Lady's husband.

Oddly, Gisela seemed more furious about her leaving than she ought to be, by rights. A kitchen girl could be replaced, but there was no doubt she was angry.

"Jumped-up little tart," she said, when a guard came to escort Serafina to her new assignment. Clearly, she had not been consulted. "Take her and welcome."

"I'm sorry, Ma'am," Serafina said stiffly. "I did not know of this."

"Like hell you didn't." Gisela stalked away. Serafina

exchanged a "what-did-I-do?" look with the cook, but Estella just shrugged.

"Good luck."

So, that was it for the kitchen. When the guard escorted her into the sunroom, she was not sorry.

It was well organized, all things considered, with several older ladies and numerous young girls attending the children —bright and sunny and cheerful, filled with books and games and little voices. The glass doors opened onto a brick patio full of planters of exotic plants, but both the glass and the vases risked injury to the children, so someone had to be aware and taking precautions at all times. Serafina soon realized that was going to be her.

It would mean riding herd on every child big enough to walk, being on her feet all day and seeming to hear the patter of little feet even at night, in her dreams. But Jalal was unmistakably tired and moody, less interested in producing little feet of her own. She supposed he might have troubles at work, but if so, he did not confide in her. She also made more money than he did and wondered if it bothered him, but again he would not say.

And there was obviously not going to be any other apartment. He was no longer interested. She was happy enough now going to work. It was preferable to being at home. The Seat was enormous and amazing, like a well-oiled machine, the beating heart of Xanthus. It would have taken her a year to explore all its corridors and outbuildings, its stables and storerooms, its banquet halls and gardens and the huge dome of the Empiricum where members met, but she wasn't permitted there anyway.

The one garden where she could go was the maze—a whimsical place of tall, trimmed hedges winding in a perplexing order few people knew, but the children loved it. When they and their caretakers had become sufficiently lost, a guard could always be depended upon to appear and guide them out, so none of the little ones were frightened. In the background, one could hear the fountains that had been turned on for summer, while lemon and orange trees framed the perimeter. It was a magical place, enough to take her mind off the grim little one where she actually lived.

It was the time when couriers came to and from the Seat, foreign dignitaries visited, and the Emperator and sometimes his Lady were seen coming and going as well. Serafina lived for those moments. Although she couldn't get close, she could see that he was a big man, probably in his forties, with iron gray hair as curly as hers, courtesy of his Omani blood. His wife, a native-born Omani, was small and slender. Her hair was still jet, usually worn swept up, which emphasized her classic profile. Beautiful and elegant, she was the envy of every kitchen and ladies maid in the Seat.

"By the gods," Patria confided one day, watching with her from outside the maze as their betters departed from the Seat in a horse drawn carriage in deference to Lady Guilia. When the Emperator went alone, he rode. "He is twice my age and I would take that man in a heartbeat."

Serafina had to stifle a giggle. "Really?"

Patria was stunningly attractive with her ruby hair, bright blue eyes and skin as fair as milk, so Serafina knew she would have no trouble attracting his notice. But it was said he was a family man, devoted to his wife and children.

"Oh, you haven't seen him close up," the other girl insisted. "If ever there was a man who is a man, he is it."

"Is that why they call him Father of Omana?" Serafina wondered.

"I wouldn't be surprised. Honestly, he has this...presence. Very, very powerful."

"Well, he is the Emperator," Serafina said. To her, that explained it. He had unlimited power, vast wealth, influence in the highest quarters of every land. He was related to most kings of the known world. His Havacian cousin was the one who kept her country subjugated. His cousin's wife was Omani, daughter of one of their most powerful Nobles, and it was said the Emperator had engineered that marriage. He had saved Xanthus from being burned to the ground during the Havacian invasion and become a hero to most of its people.

Of course he was powerful.

"He is kind, too," Patria said. "He could take a sword to the neck of anybody in this country and never be held to account for it, but he doesn't. When he hanged those who tried to kill him, he paid support to their families. He could have killed them, too."

Yet he slaughtered Domidians like flies, Serafina thought, but she said nothing. She had heard that the Havacians had gone berserk, cutting out men's hearts still beating, raping women and running over people in the streets like they were just objects. What they had done to Jalal had scarred him for life. She knew that was why her plans frightened him. He was still afraid of those people. She really should be kinder to him.

She turned away to mind the children, no longer quite so enthralled with the sight of the Emperator.

* * *

She recovered from her antipathy. Paradoxically, if Jalal thought to curtail her activities by refusing to engage with her—bedding her only infrequently, refusing to look for an apartment, remaining surly—he only made her more determined. He should know better, Serafina told herself. He knew her. If he sought to control her, he should know it was doomed to fail.

She never opposed him openly, keeping the apartment clean, not complaining, cooking as bountifully as anyone could on the shared stove in the courtyard. When he did choose to share the bed with her, she responded eagerly. She still loved that part, just not his brooding. Surely, she thought, if she was tender and passionate with him, he would come back to her as he had done at the beginning. And if he did not, it was his choice. They were not married. The city was full of young men. She could have her pick.

The problem was that when Domidian women did that, their men frequently killed them. He had never shown any inclination to harm her, but she knew them by reputation and Jalal was decidedly Domidian. He would not change.

She was the one who was changing.

More and more, she felt a sense of homecoming at the Seat, which was preposterous. That place had nothing to do with her; she was only a cog in its ever-turning wheel. But she began to realize the difference between that and other seats of power, at least by reputation. Other courts were scandal-ridden, for the most part—some of them utterly cruel. In Xanthus, people found little to criticize. The sense of a family home pervaded it despite the political intrigue always underlying the surface, as it did anywhere that men held power. Lady Guilia was more of an influence than most people realized.

Patria idolized her.

"I hope she visits again soon, then you can see for yourself," she told Serafina one day. They sat by the glass doors with a toddler apiece in their laps, waiting to intercept others who might dash for the doors during their free playtime. They were basically a net to catch bouncing balls.

"Does she often?" Serafina inquired, shaking rattles for the drooling baby held crooked in her elbow. The mothers sometimes visited during their work hours, at least briefly, and she knew this little one belonged to a chambermaid. Lady Guilia did not seem to make any distinction, insisting that all their children be cared for while the mothers worked. No one had ever heard of such a thing, but what Lady Guilia wanted, Lady Guilia got.

"No," Patria said, regretfully. "Just enough to see things are going smoothly, I suspect. After all, it was her idea. But she has a very full schedule."

Most Noble ladies did, so Serafina nodded.

"Also, she takes time to paint," Patria added.

Serafina had heard this, so she just made a noise of inquiry.

"She was always an artist," her friend explained. "From a colony on our western coast, by the sea. They were raided by Domidians." She glanced at Serafina as if anxious not to be overheard, and with her next words, Serafina understood why.

"They say she was abducted and cruelly used by Domidian men."

"Oh, my gods," Serafina said quietly. No matter their countries, any woman should have sympathy for that.

"It is common knowledge," Patria explained, "though not openly discussed. Not usually, anyway. When she met and married the Emperator, the old cows married to Empiratis tried to use it against her. They even said Dario was not his child. She removed part of her clothes at a public banquet, showed them the scars where men had beaten her and asked them what they had sacrificed for Omana."

Serafina's shocked gasp was also half laughter. This was a woman after her own heart. She didn't think even she would have had that much courage.

"I *must* meet her," she said.

Patria smiled. "Perhaps, one day. Her daughter likes to

play with the children sometimes. She is too young now, but of course we all wonder where she will be pledged."

"What of the son?" Serafina wondered.

"Well, you saw him," Patria said. "He looks enough like his mother that the Magistris finally got a handsome one."

She grinned at Serafina over the curly brunette head of the child in her arms, who was busy toothlessly worrying the bracelet on her arm. "They aren't beautiful, but they govern well."

That all depended on whom they governed, Serafina supposed. But she never played up her Domidian blood. That was still a mistake, in Omana. Jalal would never adapt and it might keep him from ever being able to do what he sought. She had hoped to be able to make inquiries about work at the Seat for him, but that was looking increasingly unlikely in the face of his attitude. She, on the other hand, embraced the necessity of blending in.

That, she thought with a flash of insight, was what was eating at him. She was doing better than he was--a thing his male pride had trouble accepting. He had made a couple of friends among the teamsters, Domidian men of the sort she had disliked serving at the caravanserai, but she had done it with a smile because it was business. Here, she did it without a smile, only to be reprimanded by Jalal because she had not been nice to his friends.

Her friends were Omanis. She wanted better living quarters, which he no longer seemed to care about. She was advancing; he was not. What was it he had said? They didn't want the same things.

She sighed and Patria looked at her questioningly.

"Trouble with my husband," she explained.

"You are not married by Omani law," Patria said, shrewdly. "We do not recognize your gods."

Serafina would not admit that they were not married by any law. That was her business.

"If he gives you too much trouble, leave him," her friend counseled. "You could do much better."

Serafina's conscience stabbed her. He had not abducted her, when he could have. He had not abandoned her on their way to Xanthus, nor in the haboob nor at the border where he could have turned back. She could not leave him.

"He has been faithful to me," she explained. "Jalal is a good man. I think he just finds it difficult to live here."

"He sounds like desert," Patria observed.

It was vaguely an insult, although Serafina did not think her friend meant it that way. To Omanis, desert meant someone who was still not quite civilized, unwilling or unable to adapt to their way of life, good for hunting and hawking and trekking with caravans, but hopeless otherwise. They were wild things that couldn't be contained and prone to rebellion because of it. The Emperator had killed any number of them because they were a threat to his reign.

Desert was not a good thing to be. If Jalal thought he might have to leave her because she was a danger, he had it the wrong way around. He was the one who might be dangerous to her.

If she thought about it, it would break her heart, so she didn't think. Instead, she worked and waited. Her time would come.

CHAPTER 16

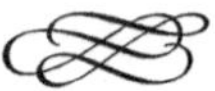

Serafina had wondered if she would see things like snow and hail in Xanthus, but people told her that was rare and exciting so far south. Instead, winter came in damp and dank and cold, with frequent lines of rain that looked like silver cascading from the sky. The residents of their building pooled funds to buy firewood that they stored in an outdoor shed so that every tenant had to haul it up two or three flights of steps to build fires in heaters so rusted that she was convinced someone would burn the place down at any moment. To wash, you heated water on top of the heater, which was such an effort that no one washed very much. Now she remembered Jalal's remark about the stench of the poor. Those who could went to the baths, which at least were heated by hypocausts. The only place she was warm was at the Seat and Jalal had no such luxury. When they did ship wine, and that was not as frequently—leading to a loss of pay—he was often soaked and shaking by the time he returned home.

Serafina hauled and heated water uncomplainingly, and tried to cook on their communal stove and get something to the top floor still hot, to warm him, afraid that he would take sick. It was still possible to buy food on the streets, but they had less money from his work, so she had to be careful. Many of the girls working at the Seat were in the same position. Winter was difficult for the poor, breathing smoke-filled air from rusty heaters while shuttered windows leaked cold air in more successfully than they funneled smoke out.

One morning there was a substantial stir in the hallway near the play room and as she watched the doorway, wondering at the commotion, a couple of guards entered. Behind them was the graceful figure of Lady Guilia.

The Lady Consort was garbed in a pale gray wool gown with an attached cape, beautifully cut and the height of fashion. Her dark hair, as usual, was swept up and secured with silver pins, she wore exquisite kid boots and a gracious smile, and the girls fell all over themselves welcoming her.

Behind her, to her consternation, Serafina spotted her nemesis. None other than Gisela the housekeeper accompanied Lady Guilia. Her look raked Serafina and she spoke quietly to her Lady. To Serafina's horror, the Emperator's wife looked at her directly, somberly, and half smiled.

She nodded as she had seen other girls do, as the Lady approached her, only to have that august personage reach out, gently raising her chin, searching her face.

"You are new here, are you not?"

She was nearly too intimidated to reply, but finally croaked, "Yes, Lady Guilia."

"What is your name, dear?"

"Serafina, Ma'am." In the background, Gisela was glowering at her. What offense could she possibly have given?

"I see. And you are from Domidia?"

Well, that was probably it. Most likely Gisela had told her. And surely this woman had no reason to love Domidians.

"Yes, Ma'am."

"Which part?"

"Someno, Ma'am."

"Ah, Someno. I see." Lady Guilia spoke quietly, with no particular inflection, yet for some reason that was of interest, as it had been to Gisela. Serafina wracked her brain trying to think of anything notable about Someno, anything, but nothing came to mind.

Luckily, the Lady seemed to lose interest after that, stepping back and surveying the room.

"The children look well," she complimented the ladies in total. "I know the rain and cold are hard on some of you and I have asked Gisela to provide hot breakfast and dinner for each of you, at least until the weather improves."

There was a round murmur of surprise and gratitude.

"Also, if any of you are short of firewood, see the house guard, Marcellus. He will have a bundle for anyone who asks."

This woman really was a wonder, Serafina thought. She knew of no one who would make any such concessions to the poor, other than the ladies of the Temple, and those were seeking converts. She had not been desperate enough to go to them, but she would take Lady Guilia's offerings, gladly. There was nothing at all this wealthy, elegant woman wanted from her, aside from her labor, and that was not onerous. The children could tire one out, but it was easy compared to the heavy lifting, chopping and running of the kitchen.

She had thought herself exempt from attention after the Lady's brief questions, but the Emperator's wife turned to her again, speaking quietly. "Please come with me."

She turned without looking further, expecting immediate obedience, and Serafina had only time to glance desperately at Patria, but her friend merely shrugged. Serafina felt every eye in the room boring into her back as she followed Lady Guilia and the man she now recognized as Captain of the

Guard, Bonifaci. Good gods, had Jalal been right and she was already on her way to prison? But she had said nothing to anyone of her intentions. How could they know?

To her surprise, Lady Guilia turned to Gisela as they stepped into the hall. "Please leave us."

And then to Serafina, "Come with me."

Serafina could feel herself breaking out into a cold sweat, proceeding with the Lady and her guard down long marble corridors where she had never been or thought to be. Braziers heated the halls, while they passed priceless statuary, crystal and paintings that must have cost a fortune. For a moment, she wondered if Lady Guilia had painted any of them, but of course it was more suitable for a lady to paint portraits rather than the broad sweeping scenic canvases they passed.

After what seemed an eternity of pacing after the silent Captain, he ushered her through carved oak doors into a chamber in which Lady Guilia had preceded her. Then, without comment, he stepped back into the hallway, closing the doors, and Serafina was alone with the Royal Consort.

The Lady turned to her again with her enigmatic half smile. "Please," she said, "don't be afraid. You have done nothing wrong. I just wished to speak to you in private."

"Yes, Ma'am, "Serafina replied, still utterly dumbfounded.

"Tea?" her Lady inquired.

A tea set rested on a cherry table before a fireplace for which she and Jalal would have sold their souls. They hadn't been warm in ages and she shuddered to think of him, sometimes, out in the rain and the muck being worked without mercy. She knew they treated him like shit on his job, while she was being offered tea in the Seat.

"Thank you, Ma'am," she stuttered.

Lady Guilia poured tea as if she had been doing it all her life, setting it along with a plate of biscuits on a table in front of one of her brocade couches facing the fireplace. The room had a very lived-in feel, as if she was there frequently. "Please sit. Are you cold?"

"Oh, no, Ma'am," Serafina replied, sinking into a sumptuous couch. "They keep us well supplied in the play room."

It was the truth. She was warm and fed all day while Jalal worked for a pittance, soaked to the skin. She could hardly blame him for his lack of enthusiasm about anything.

"Yes, well, of course the children are there." The Lady smiled, pouring for herself and also taking a seat. "They seem in very good order."

"I believe so, Ma'am," Serafina replied, sipping cautiously. No one had to tell her this was the most expensive tea money could buy, no doubt brought by ship and then caravan to Xanthus. The biscuits were some of Gisela's best. She knew, because at one time she had helped bake them.

"Well, tell me a little more, if you will. How long have you been in Xanthus?"

"Only a few weeks, Lady."

"And before that?"

"On a caravan. My husband and I went north from Someno and then over the border and with another one to get here."

Lady Guilia raised her brows. "That is a very long trip. You must have wanted to come very badly."

"There is little opportunity in Domidia," Serafina replied, relaxing fractionally.

"You are married?"

This was one person she would not lie to.

"Only in the common way," she admitted. "You have none of our priests here."

"I see." There was no least inflection in the Lady's speech. "And before that? What did you do?"

"I worked in the caravanserai. In Someno. They have a rather large one there."

"Yes, so I have heard. Did you work for someone there, or have merchandise?"

Serafina wondered if she was going to be given another job other than the play room.

"My mother had the merchandise, she had a stall there. But I helped her with everything, the ordering and selling and stocking. I had to learn several languages and all of the money. We had customers from every country."

If she was being sought for a job, she might as well spell out her qualifications.

The Lady paused, sipping for a moment. "What is your mother's name?"

"Pescia, Ma'am."

Abruptly, Lady Guilia replaced her cup in its saucer, looking closely at her.

"Pescia. In Someno. In the market."

"Yes, Ma'am."

This was such a puzzling conversation, Serafina could make no sense of it, nor of the fact that her Lady rose silently, going to the opposite side of the room where there was another set of doors. They opened silently. Beyond the portal, Serafina could see a large canopied bed, and she realized with a shock that she was in the private living quarters of the Emperator. No wonder Lady Guilia had dismissed Gisela. She would have a stroke.

"I think you should come in," the Emperator's wife said into the room.

Serafina blinked. Fate had delivered exactly what she requested squarely into her lap. The Emperator was the person in the other room and entered, filling the doorway, smiling at his wife.

Patria was right, she thought in her one moment of clarity. This was a man—large, bold featured, dressed as if he might at any moment take horse and ride into his Empire, in boots and spurs, leather pantaloons, a doublet and tunic. All he lacked was a helmet and a sword. She could believe everything she had heard of him and that he had terrified the Domidians. He terrified her.

Yet when he spoke, his voice was warm. Warm and deep. She had heard he had a manner that charmed the citizens when he spoke to them and now she heard it for herself.

"You are Pescia's daughter?"

"Y-yes."

He stopped right in front of her, looking down at her in the light of the fire and several oil lamps while Lady Guilia seated herself again, utterly silent. In a moment, he took the other chair, not looming over her.

"When were you born, Serafina?"

"Six and ten years ago," she replied. "It was just after the war. I don't remember it, though."

"No, of course not." The Emperator helped himself to a biscuit. "What else do you remember?"

"Um...nothing special," she said. "My mother sold fruit, then other things. Her cousin Imrun helped her."

"Oh, I'm quite sure he did." The Emperator's tone was dry. "Is he still alive?"

"Yes."

He shrugged. "Waiting for her to die, no doubt."

It sounded almost as if he knew Imrun.

"Yes," she admitted. "That is exactly what he is doing. He sought to marry me to his clerk so that stall would pass to him."

The Emperator looked at her, gimlet-eyed.

"And you refused?"

"Yes."

"But she is here with someone." Lady Guilia put in quietly.

"Oh?"

You did not stay silent when the Emperator said, "Oh."

"He is a friend since childhood. Well, actually, he is the one they wanted me to marry."

He chuckled. "So instead you ran away with him to Omana, do I have that right?"

"Well, yes. I didn't dislike him, I just refused to be bullied."

"And where is he?"

"Working today, I hope." Serafina's fingers were trembling on the handle of her bone china teacup.

"You are not in trouble," Emperator Sergius reassured her, as his wife had done. "We simply wanted to know more about you."

"You are satisfied?" Lady Guilia inquired of him, and he nodded.

"Yes, this is the girl."

What girl? Suddenly, Serafina was convinced he knew her father's identity. It was why she was being questioned. She held her breath in hope. All they had to do was tell her and then she would go away forever, if they wished.

Instead, he smiled at her. "You have my mother's eyes."

She knew she had Havacian eyes, which had been remarked upon all her life. That was why the full implication of what he had said did not sink in at first. When it did, she just sucked in her breath, unable to speak.

"Hers are more blue," he went on, unperturbed, "but they are hers, all the same. I would know them anywhere. As for the rest, you are a Magistri, plain as day. It is no wonder that Gisela knew."

"Knew what?" she finally croaked.

"That you are my daughter," the Emperator said. "I met

your mother during the war. You are mine." He bent forward, briefly stroking down her cheek with one thumb.

"You even look like one of our women. Not pretty like all the young girls want to be, but beautiful as women are. You will be a woman longer than you will ever be a girl, and you will still be beautiful."

Immediately, she glanced at the Lady, whose expression told her she knew and had probably known for a long time.

"Yours? You slept with my mother?"

He looked straight at her. "Yes, I am the one."

"And you sent the money?"

"Yes." He reached over for a moment, resting his hand on Lady Guilia's knee. "You are my daughter. I owed you that much."

"It's true, Serafina," the Lady said. "I have known about you for years. It happened before I ever met your father. We just never dreamed you would come here."

"Are you angry?" Serafina half whispered.

"Angry? No." Her father munched another biscuit thoughtfully. "It is exactly what I would have done."

Serafina thought she might be sick. Emotions were swirling inside her so ferociously that she didn't think she could contain them. The Emperator, her father. That was what Jadda had meant. She had known.

"Ummi never told me," she said softly. "She never said."

Sergius Magistri stood up again, hands in his tunic pockets. She thought for just a moment that he might be nearly as disconcerted as she was. Lady Guilia was the only one who was glacially calm.

"That was our arrangement," he finally said. "Your mother could never come here and so we parted, but not before I had seen you. I told her I would provide for you, and I did."

The thought seemed to give him pause. "Where are you living now?"

"By the docks, near the winery."

He shook his head. "Unacceptable. I would not house a rat in those places."

She just waited in silence for him to tell her what would become of her life. He had the power. He had every power. He could kill her, hide her, do anything to her, and to Jalal, as well. Gods, what had she done?

"Your friend is there, as well?"

"Of course," she said.

"Loyal," he commented. "Well, I would have expected no less. Do you love this man?"

She stared at her feet. "I am not sure."

"And yet you stay with him," Lady Guilia said gently.

"I cannot leave him."

"Are you afraid of him?" the Emperator asked at once.

"Jalal? No! He would never harm me."

"I am glad you think so," he said, a trifle grimly. "Domidian men do not have a good reputation that way."

"He would never share me with anyone else, I know," she replied, remembering their conversation after she had been in the baths. "But he would not hurt me, either."

"Oh, my love, you are so young," Lady Guilia breathed. "It is hardly possible for you to know what you want."

"She knows what she wants," the Emperator corrected. "She's here, isn't she?"

Lady Guilia smiled. "She is, at that."

"Well, you cannot be known as yet," the Emperator decided, "and you cannot remain in that rat hole. As far as anyone knows, you will be one of Lady Guilia's ladies. You will live here; we will give you a small chamber and if you want your friend there—although I do not like it—he can come."

"He is very good with horses, My Lord," she replied, anxiously. "Could he not work in your stables?"

"Is that what he does now?"

"Partly," she said. "More so they just use him for any dirty job they care to. He has been poorly treated. I am not sure how much more of Omana he will want. He may leave, I think."

"That depends on how much he wants you," her father informed her. "We will offer and he can decide. Some may guess who you are; Gisela already knows. I must tell our children, which will not be easy. But it is better for you than what you have."

It was—inestimably better. If only Jalal would agree. But even if he would not, Serafina knew, she was staying. She had found her father. She would not easily let him go.

CHAPTER 17

She tried to decline when they told her Bonifaci would accompany her to her lodgings, because she still feared him, but her father shook his head.

"I use Bonifaci because I can trust him," he averred. "So can you."

She thought it was a sad statement, implying that there were so many he could not trust, but said nothing. And so the captain of the Emperator's Havacian Guard—himself an Omani—accompanied her through the streets of Xanthus. Cloaked against the rain, he was not identifiable as such, but Serafina could virtually feel the leashed power in this man. Short, solid, pock-marked and totally imperturbable, he inquired only if she could ride and, when she nodded, had three horses brought. They, too, were plainly attired, not wearing the customary red and yellow checked livery of the Emperator. As far as anyone knew, they were a soldier and a girl riding in the rain.

It was teeming down when they reached the apartment, with everyone holed up inside and some pathetic smoke swirling out the one stovepipe on top of the building before being obliterated by rain.

"Who's that?" Bonifaci asked, and Serafina made out the figures of two men coming from their apartment. They were the two Domidians with whom Jalal had established a loose sort of friendship.

"Oh, there you are," one said rudely. "Better go look after him."

"What's wrong?" Serafina asked. "Did the horses hurt him?"

The first one shook his head, throwing off water like a wet dog. "Nah. He's sick. Sick enough they let us bring him home."

No one let sick Domidians come home from a day's work. They worked them until they dropped. She cast an anguished look at her father's captain, who immediately tossed a coin to the man who had spoken.

"Watch our horses." Otherwise, they would be stolen. He followed as she ran two at a time up the wet, slippery steps.

They had not locked the door. She burst inside, heading immediately for the bed where she knew he would be. The apartment was freezing because you could not let the stoves burn while you worked. Jalal was a bulky figure beneath blankets, face turned away from her, and she sat on the edge of the bed. He didn't move and she looked up helplessly at the captain. For all she knew, his friends had delivered a corpse. He wouldn't be the first one. People had died in that complex before.

Bonifaci turned him, one hand beneath his head, and Jalal stirred.

"You're home," he said, focusing on Serafina. "Who's he?"

"A friend of my father's," she said.

"You found your father?"

"Yes." She reached beneath the blanket, feeling his tunic,

which was soaked. The moment she touched his chest, he coughed—a long, wracking cough that made her look up anxiously into Bonifaci's less than beautiful face.

"Lung fever," he said, shortly. "He can't stay here."

"What?" Jalal protested, but the guard was already picking him up, blanket and all, slinging him over his shoulder like a sack of grain, holding him by his legs.

"Get your things," Bonifaci said, heading for the door.

As Serafina threw their few possessions into their bedrolls, a habit learned on the caravan that she now blessed, he simply took Jalal like a package down the treacherous stairs until Jalal's two friends took him bodily at the bottom.

"Get him on the horse," Bonifaci instructed, and they hoisted him onto the snorting cavalry mount they had brought for him. Serafina ran down the steps behind them, the straps of their bedrolls looped around her neck while their possessions whacked her in the behind with every step.

Jalal was not protesting, by which she knew that he was seriously ill.

"Here," Bonifaci said, running a length of leather around his ankles and beneath the horse to the other ankle, then tucking his arms through the martingale all cavalry mounts wore. He glanced at Serafina and at her horse. "Get up."

Despite her reassurance to Bonifaci, she had seldom ridden a horse. But wherever he was taking Jalal, she was going. One of his friends, seeing her hesitate, boosted her onto the tall mount, but then he ruined any impression of friendship.

"If'n 'e don't come back, can we have yer stove?"

Technically, it belonged to their landlord, but she knew they would never be back and it wasn't the first time an empty apartment had been rifled. "Suit yourself," she said.

Bonifaci stripped off his cloak, tucking it around Jalal, securing the edges beneath his arms and legs. He was coughing again, the same wet, wracking coughs she had heard in the apartment. The captain was right, she thought in panic, it was lung fever, which took so many lives in winter. This was what she had feared.

The Emperator's guard swung up on his horse. His uniform was visible, making him more identifiable, but no one would trouble them in the downpour. Without a word to Jalal's friends, he put spurs to his horse, taking the rein to Jalal's horse because he would be incapable of using it, and led them through streets running and gurgling with rain.

There was not the usual bustle at the Seat to see their odd progress, for which she was profoundly grateful, but no one would question the Emperator's captain in any case. Heart in her throat, she saw that Bonifaci was taking them around to the back, to the same door she had entered her first day at the Seat.

"Oh, no," she said quietly. They would enter by the kitchen, the last place she wanted to be. Two guards stood partially sheltered in the casement, but stood to attention when they saw their captain, who jumped down with only a few words.

"Got someone here the Lady wants taken care of," he said. "Take him to the small chamber by the dairy room."

It was by far the most remote part of the Seat to which Serafina had ever been and she heaved a sigh of partial relief. The other two men unstrapped Jalal from his horse, taking him between them in a sort of chair-carry into the stone kitchens, through and then out. Well, so much for invisibility. Serafina could see the kitchen girls gawking at them, but no one gainsaid Bonifaci, who strode through as if he would obliterate anyone in his way. Serafina knew people feared him. He was said to give no quarter in battle and hardly any to civilians, but just then he was her friend.

"Here, you," he said to her, as if he hardly knew her, as the men carried Jalal in. "You can take care of him. Get water, tell Gisela you want the physician. Get on it, now."

Well, he had spoken to her—fittingly—as a servant. Her reputation was intact for the moment. She fled to the kitchen, where the staff clustered, Gisela looking like thunder in the midst of them.

"Captain Bonifaci wants the physician," she said breathlessly. "And warm water. I will take it."

"You heard her," Gisela said nastily to one of the girls, who fled, presumably to fetch the Emperator's physician. "Who've you got there, then?"

Serafina just shrugged. "Someone they want kept alive. I'm to tend him."

"How's that?" a strange voice inquired, and she looked up into the face of Prince Dario. Apparently, he had been whiling away an idle hour making chat with one of the more comely kitchen maids and Serafina cursed her luck.

"I'll take it," he said as one of the girls lugged up a bucket of water filled from the caldron they kept heated at all times.

"Come on," he said to Serafina.

Apparently, he knew his way to the hidden bed chamber. Even hampered by the bucket, he still outpaced Serafina and she had to trot to keep up.

"So you are my sister," he said beneath his breath as she pulled even with him.

She just looked at him, dumbstruck and afraid. He didn't sound particularly friendly. "All the way from Domidia," he added.

"Yes," she quavered.

"A good scandal, if it gets out." His tone was scathing. "I warn you, sister or not, if you use this to hurt my parents, I'll make you regret you were ever born."

Looking at his profile, she knew he meant it. That was a resolute young man if ever she had seen one. He would be

Emperator one day. He had to be that way and, apparently, he was starting young.

"I won't hurt them," she said. "I wanted nothing from them, just to know who my father was. I never suspected it was him."

"Oh, didn't you?" He put the bucket down outside the door, leaving it for her to take it the rest of the way. "That's why you came to the Seat, I suppose, because you had no idea."

"I didn't!" she protested. "I just thought from something my grandmother said that he knew who it was. I only wanted to ask, that's all."

"Well, now you've kicked up a proper hornet's nest," he said. "And who is this the cat dragged in, your lover?"

"Yes!" she said, losing her temper. "And he wants nothing from you, either. He wouldn't bother."

She picked up the bucket, staggering under its weight.

"Good," her brother said, and walked away.

Inside, Bonifaci had competently started a fire in the brazier, stripped the wet clothes off Jalal and kicked out the two guards before they could learn any more. He looked up at her entrance. Jalal was not moving.

"Sponge him with the warm water," he instructed. "Just move the blanket as you work and then cover him again. He needs to be warmed up, quickly."

Following his instructions, she set to work, seeing the sense of it, praying for the physician to come. Jalal looked barely conscious, his eyelids fluttering occasionally, choking at times with suppressed coughs.

Above her, Bonifaci surprised her by pushing Jalal's soaked hair back off his forehead, examining his face.

"He's just a boy," he said, as if surprised. "How did you two make it from Domidia?"

"With difficulty," she said grimly, sponging. "But it took Omana to kill him."

"I have seen those who lived through the haboob get this, later," the Captain said. "The sand gets in their lungs. He's not dead yet. People recover from lung fever. Not easily, but they have lived."

Serafina looked at up him, cautiously hopeful because it was the only hope she had. Jalal had been bad when she left in the morning, but now he looked terrible.

"He's got fever," Bonifaci said, hand on his forehead. "When they don't, they die. It means the body quit."

"He won't quit," Serafina said, fiercely.

"I hope not." Bonifaci might have said more, but just then the physician came in, a thin, ascetic-looking man Serafina had only glimpsed once before. This was the Emperator's own physician, she thought in awe. If he could not save Jalal, no one could.

"Very good," he said, smiling at her efforts. "He is warmer already, I'm sure." Cautiously, he pulled back the blankets, pressing an ear to Jalal's chest, listening intently.

"The lungs are inflamed, of course, but the heart is strong. He is young. He has a good chance."

"Then I must go," Bonifaci said. "This girl will care for him."

"So I see," the doctor mused, looking at her expression.

"It is to be kept quiet," the captain warned the other man, who nodded.

"I understand."

Serafina had no idea how much he did understand, but no doubt these people had a network among them. She was in the inner workings of the Seat now, like it or not. And Jalal was there and she knew he was not going to like it, but there was no choice. He would have died in their apartment. Here, at least he had a chance.

Unless her brother killed him, of course, Serafina thought ironically. He had looked angry enough to kill and she knew nothing of his character. Still, if he sought to protect his parents, who could blame him? An illegitimate child intent on wreaking havoc or emptying the treasury or enjoining plots was a real danger. But she was none of those things.

All she wanted was for Jalal to live.

She slept little for the next few days and no one asked her to work. She saw nothing of the Emperator or the Lady, and thankfully nothing of Dario, but guards arrived periodically with meals and whatever else she asked them to bring. These were the Emperator's men, who would keep his secrets, not servants who would gossip.

Watching Jalal, she knew he was fighting for his life. He had always done it, she thought ruefully—living through invasion, surviving the deplorable camps, being taken in by Imrun only to be used like someone indentured, working for meals and a bed. Now he was in Omana, where he was viewed as the enemy when all he wanted was a job. He had wanted her as a wife and she had refused him, only sharing his bed. How much did he really have to live for? Yet he fought, with the same determination that had carried both of them from Domidia. She knew she could never have done it without him.

And so she cared for him with total purpose, sponging him when he sweated, warming him with her body when he shook with chills, trickling water and soup into his mouth when he was conscious enough to swallow, lying by the hour beside him when he was not. The physician came periodically, saying very little, leaving medicines for him. Using the knowledge given by her mother, Serafina prepared plasters she spread on his chest to draw the poison from his lungs. They seemed to work, making him cough until she was afraid it would break the frame of the bed, or his ribs. She held him then, thumping his back to clear his lungs as she remembered Ummi doing when she was a child, making him breathe in steam from kettles of boiling water she asked guards to bring.

On the third day, the physician looked up at her with a wintry smile, listening intently to Jalal's breathing and his heart.

"Better," he said. "I think we are making progress. There is nothing like good nursing care."

Jalal stirred, pulling away from someone he recognized as Omani.

"Jalal, hush," Serafina said gently. "He is helping you."

He stopped, focusing on her with difficulty. "Where are we?"

"At the Seat," she replied, looking at the doctor, who silently packed his medications and left. "They have let us have a room so I can care for you here. You've had lung fever."

"I know that," he said, beginning to be irascible, and she smiled.

"You're getting better," she encouraged him.

"Why would they do that?" he wondered.

Serafina took a deep breath, easing him back down onto the pillows they had piled so that he slept half sitting, the better to clear his lungs.

"I found my father," she said. "You were right, he has influence. That is why we are here."

"Who is he?"

She steeled herself, unable to predict even to herself how he would respond.

"The Emperator."

"What?" He looked stunned, just as she had felt.

"It's true. He met my mother on one of the campaigns.

They agreed Mummi would never say who he was and he sent money."

"And now he knows who you are?"

"Yes."

He just shook his head, framed against a mountain of pillows. "Fool. You are in it now."

"In what?" she protested. "He has been very kind."

"In whatever happens," Jalal predicted. Conscious again, he was thinking. "Men like that have enemies, which means now you have them, too."

Serafina shook her head. "I'm inconsequential. Just a by-blow. I'm lucky he has a good nature, that's all."

"Does he? I wonder."

She pulled his cover up, standing. "Well, don't wonder, sleep. You've been half dead. We have a good situation here, so just rest." But she bent to stroke the side of his face, smiling at him. "Your beard needs trimming. Get a little sleep and I will do it for you."

She hesitated, wondering if it was the right time. Probably there never would be one, so she just bent over him, taking his hand, squeezing his fingers. "I have to take good care of you. You are going to be a father."

She had nearly been sick in the Lady's sitting room and queasy ever since, which she had attributed to nerves. Then she had thought during their stay how grateful she was for inside accommodations so that she need not use the communal, outdoor latrine that had been a nightmare, especially during her courses. And then she had realized she had not had any.

"You're pregnant?" Jalal asked.

She nodded. "I will ask that physician, but yes, I think so."

He closed his eyes as if wanting to ignore the information and she tried to tell herself it was just that he was sick.

Outside, birds were waking, fluttering by the windows

that were barred because they were at ground level. Emperators did have enemies. Her father's had tried to kill him. Jalal could be absolutely right. He usually was.

"Women do get pregnant, you know," she said.

She was repeating her mother's history, having a child at the worst possible time by a man who probably did not want it.

"Yes," he said. "They do."

He opened his eyes, looking into her face. He had beautiful eyes, dark and deep. Suddenly, it reminded her of the night she had lain with him, spent after lovemaking, when he had told her she still didn't know him.

There were depths to Jalal, she was realizing, that no one knew. But she wanted to.

"Just get better," she whispered, bending over him. "Please."

CHAPTER 18

In the sitting room he sometimes shared with his wife, the Emperator of Omana was drinking a fine, aged brandy. She was not there, because she was angry with him.

Well, he couldn't blame her. All the deeds of his misspent youth were piling up, coming back to haunt him. Being arguably the most powerful man in the world did not exempt him from family problems. Now, he had an angry wife, a wayward pregnant daughter, confused children and a prospective son-in-law who looked just like men he had killed and inspired the same feeling in him. And as word of the situation trickled out, as it was bound to do, he would probably have even worse problems.

Taking another swig, he began to laugh. Life was absurd. He had always known it. The trick was learning to weave your way through it, like a drunk in a maze. He had been doing it for years. This was just another test.

There was a discreet knock at the door. Recognizing it, he called, "Come."

The increasing bulk of his adjutant, Semet the Havacian,

showed in the doorway. Semet had lived well during their years of peace. He might be a little slower with the sword, but not in his wits. Sergius kicked away a small lady's stool, clearing the way to a couch the big Havacian would fill.

"Sit down," he invited. "I'm toasting myself."

"To what?" Semet inquired. But he took the seat and the flask of brandy the Emperator passed to him.

"Congratulate me, I'm to be a grandfather."

To his credit, Semet did not choke. "Not Dario, I hope."

Sergius waved a hand vaguely. "No, no, he knows better. Unlike me at that age. No, it is my long-lost daughter and that little Domidian son of a bitch."

"Ow." Semet drank.

"Exactly." His Emperator sighed. "Five and ten years I've worked to have a somewhat respectable reputation and here it goes."

"Well, you're not the one who's pregnant," Semet pointed out.

Sergius shook his head. "Can't blame the girl. She's getting by as best she can, the same as her mother did. I'm the cause of this."

"Just because you knocked up a girl a thousand miles away?"

"Yes. A soldier can do that. An Emperator can't."

"You were a soldier then," Semet opined. "Anyone who objects now can eat my sword or Bonifaci's, take their pick."

"An appealing prospect," Sergius admitted. "I wouldn't mind killing someone right now."

Semet stared into the fireplace, well supplied with wood brought from private forests belonging to the Empire. "Where can you send her?"

"Nowhere," Sergius said. "She's too far gone. She's so damn innocent, I don't think she even knew for a while. That boy picked the fruit right off the vine."

"Domidian son of a bitch," Semet sympathized again. He, too, had killed them by the score.

"Took advantage of a girl too young to know better," Sergius agreed. "She's a child having a child. I've put her to work attending Guilia and him in the stables, but that's only for now."

"Is Guilia killing you over this?"

"She's not pleased, of course, but no. We had this out years ago, when I told her about Pescia. I think she's mostly gotten over it, it's just dredging up some residual damage."

He smiled, gesturing to Semet to pass back the flask.

"She's too decent to take it out on Serafina."

"You never did it again, did you?" Semet asked.

Sergius shook his head. "Never."

"Too bad Bonifaci couldn't say he was too sick to move and left him till he died," Semet said.

Sergius guffawed. "You think like a Havacian. He's Omani. His orders were to bring Jalal to the Seat, so he brought him to the Seat."

"So honorable," Semet said, sourly.

They were both silent for a moment.

"Well, he's here now," Sergius said, "and if I kill him, she'll love him forever, like a monument."

He looked long and deep into the fire, tapping his glass.

"I know women. They're sentimental. Guilia would like to see her married. It would suit me, too."

"To him?" Semet asked, incredulous.

"To him." Sergius nodded. "A proper, legal, unbreakable marriage. As it stands now, if she leaves him or he leaves her, some Omani officer with a pretty face and too much ambition will catch the falling apple. That could present a problem for Dario later. If Guilia sweet talks them into a marriage, no Domidian stands a chance in hell of touching this Seat, especially that one. All he wants is to raise some horses. I've got plenty of those. I'll give him all he wants. All he has to do is marry my daughter."

Semet whistled. "That's a new one, even for you."

The Emperator's face set in a fashion eerily reminiscent of his son's. "They sold my grandmother in chains, in the streets of Omana. You're damn right I'll sell her for horses. She's lucky."

He stood up, abruptly. "Come on, let's ride somewhere."

* * *

IF HER FATHER could ride his problems away, Serafina could not work hers away. She had tried, working assiduously at the less-than-arduous tasks of a lady's maid. She knew it was Lady Guilia she had to thank for her relative good fortune and was careful to attend to her every need, filling a role it had taken other women years to achieve. For that very reason, she knew the Seat was rife with rumors as to how she had done it.

She had told no one. She could have no friends or confidantes now. She had had to rebuff Patria's overtures, knowing the girl was boiling with curiosity that could prove, if not fatal, at least difficult. Her brother was openly hostile, she had not even seen her sister, and her father was conspicuous by his absence.

She wanted her mother. For the first time, she began to think it might even be better in Domidia, and she knew Jalal did, but there was no hope of returning now. She was pregnant, unable to withstand another trip of a thousand miles. This baby would have to be born in Omana, born a bastard unless one of them changed their minds.

In her heart, she had to admit her single-minded determination to find her father had ruined her life.

Only one positive thing happened. Bound to another day

of needlework in Lady Guilia's sewing room, she was picking snarls out of her thread yet again when a shadow fell across the snowy linen she was embroidering with such difficulty. She looked up, catching her breath.

In the doorway, a diffident little girl stood staring at her, big-eyed. There were many children in the Seat, but none who looked so obviously like Lady Guilia. She had her mother's dark hair, huge dark eyes and a sweet, shy expression.

"Hello," Serafina said carefully. "Are you Lissa?"

The child nodded. "Are you my sister?"

"If you are Lissa, yes. I'm Serafina."

The girl took a tentative step into the room. No doubt she had been there many times, but always with her mother and ladies. This time, there was only Serafina, who held her breath, knowing this was a crucial moment.

"I'm Lissa." She came forward shyly, peering at the work Serafina was attempting to create. "That's not how you do it."

"I'm sure it's not. Would you like to show me?"

"Like this." Quietly, the little girl took the work from her hands, sitting on the bench beside her feet, but turning to demonstrate. "First, the needle goes through. Then you wrap the thread around it three times, see? One, two, three. Pull it tight. Then put the needle back down through the cloth, very close to where it came up and tug. Just a little. Now you've got a knot."

She smiled at Serafina. "If you make a lot of them close together, you get a flower."

"I see," Serafina breathed, amazed at such skill in a child. "You're very good, you know."

Lissa promptly made another one, tucked carefully beside the first. "Well, I've been doing it a long time."

What was a long time when you were only about eight years old, Serafina wondered, but she smiled tenderly at the child. Perhaps it wouldn't be so bad, having one. She had not let herself think about it, until then, viewing it as an unwelcome disruption in her life. But it was more than that, of course, it was a child. She was beginning to feel it inside her. You couldn't deny truth. Even Jalal had admitted as much, treating her very carefully, as if she had become fragile.

"Do you like the idea of a sister?" she asked gently.

Lissa nodded, head bowed over the embroidery. Her dark hair was neatly parted down the middle, formed into two braids tied with shiny ribbon, and she wore a painstakingly pleated frock that reached to her tiny ankles. She was a child of wealth and privilege—beloved. This could have been her life, Serafina knew, but it wasn't. It was not the little girl's fault. She was only a child, and adorable. Who would not love her?

"I always wanted one," Lissa whispered. "Can we be sisters?"

Serafina bent forward, softly kissing the bent little head. The child smelled of flowers. "We already are."

CHAPTER 19

For once, Jalal seemed reasonably happy. He had coughed for weeks, but recovered slowly, until by the fall he was healthy and able to work in the cavernous stables of the Emperator, where he could remain largely unseen.

Serafina, on the other hand, could not. She was large with child, restricted in her activities and waiting for it to be over. More and more, she wanted her mother, but she counted herself fortunate that Lady Guilia seemed to take over the role. The two of them grew close, as such things could be counted.

That was why she finally listened when her Lady urged a marriage before the child came.

"I understand how you are feeling, or very nearly," she assured Serafina one absolutely splendid fall day. It was all green and gold, such a change from Domidia that Serafina was often overcome by its beauty, even in the city.

Serafina was just silent, unsure how this privileged person could ever understand the feelings of a poor shop girl from Domidia. Nevertheless, she realized, Lady Guilia tried.

She seemed to have the purest heart Serafina had ever known and now she understood how the Emperator had chosen this woman for his wife. Her mother was never going to qualify. It was not even a contest. She had been a youthful indiscretion.

"I did not want to marry, at first," Lady Guilia said, surprising her. "Oh, I loved him." She had interpreted Serafina's look. "I think I always loved him, right from the first. He found me at the worst time of my life and wouldn't let me die, it was that simple. He was decent and kind just when I needed that most—to reassure me that there was still something good in this world."

She sighed at the memory.

"But I never thought I could fulfill the obligations of a Royal Consort. It scared me to death. The sniping old ladies, the intrigues, the speeches to thousands of people, it just overwhelmed me."

"How did you do it?" Serafina wondered. Lady Guilia showed no indication of self-doubt now. She was the soul of courtesy and aplomb.

"I leaned on him. Really. Almost literally. And then we went away to Cana—that's the Emperator's family estate to the south—and it was such a magical place. It healed me, I think."

She gave a most unladylike laugh. "It was a good thing, because it was there I realized I was pregnant with Dario."

Serafina was so shocked that she stopped stitching. Her needlework was improving under the tutelage of an eight-year-old child, but that stopped her.

"You were...you did...but you were not married?"

Lady Guilia shook her head, laughing. "No. He had asked me countless times, but I was always afraid. Then I realized that I had to do it for my child's sake. I could not leave him without a name, without an acknowledged father. That is a dreadful thing for any child, but especially a boy."

Serafina knew that was true. In Domidia, boys still could be introduced as so-and-so, son of so-and-so. The old ways died hard.

"Are you saying I should marry?" she asked quietly.

"That would be up to you," Lady Guilia said. "And Jalal, of course."

"Jalal would not be a problem," Serafina admitted. "It's me."

"Then he wants it?" her Lady pried gently.

Serafina nodded. "He says it is dishonorable to go on this way and that you have magistrates."

Lady Guilia looked thoughtful. "Well, that surprises me, but he's right. You need not take any religious vows. I know we have the well-meaning ladies of the Temple, but they have no authority, they are only there for those who want them. The Emperator himself does not worship Omani gods, he worships the Northern Goddess of his mother. He goes to Temple with me only as a courtesy. Here, people are whatever they wish."

"It is not that way in Domidia," Serafina said darkly. "They kill you, if they can evade the Omanis. Secretly, in some back alley. And very badly."

The Lady blanched and Serafina could have bitten her tongue.

"I just..." she began to apologize, but Guilia interrupted her.

"I know. I am so glad you are out of there."

"The religious patrols are a curse," Serafina admitted. "Jalal hates them. Of course, you can say nothing. But he would be fine with a magistrate."

"Then will you think about it?" Guilia urged softly. "I do not think you have much time left."

Serafina didn't think so, either. She was huge and uncomfortable, having the contractions people said preceded birth, being checked nearly every day by the physician at Lady Guilia's insistence.

"How soon could we do it?"

"At a moment's notice," her father's wife assured her.

Everything at the Seat could be done at a moment's notice and frequently was, at the Emperator's pleasure or his wife's. His power was absolute, though most people liked to pretend it was not.

"I should do it," Serafina decided. "I will ask Jalal. He would come here for that, I think."

Jalal had never set foot in the Seat other than to sleep with her in their little bed chamber, using the back door. He spoke to no one, made no friends and avoided her father like disease. If he wanted badly enough to be married, though, she supposed he might come inside for a few minutes.

"I can ask," she repeated. "Can it be quiet?"

"Oh, very quiet," the Lady assured her. "We will not make him uncomfortable. He is apparently a better man than I thought. We can do it right in my sitting chamber."

Her father's very existence made him uncomfortable, but Serafina would not speak of that. Everyone knew it and she was somewhat amazed that Sergius agreed with this, but if his wife was asking, he did. Serafina had realized, not without a pang of regret for Ummi, that they loved each other deeply and were partners. If one proposed, the other disposed. This was actually coming from him.

She supposed she would have to put up with Dario, too. She only hoped he hated Domidians somewhat less than his father did. Probably the only one who would be happy was Lissa, who seemed to have given Serafina her whole heart, unquestioningly.

* * *

In the end, Dario would not come although his sister did, bearing a bouquet of flowers she handed to Serafina with a shy smile.

"Thank you, sweetheart," Serafina said, taking them carefully. They were roses, but someone had removed all the thorns.

They had given her a gown, tent-sized to accommodate her condition, and flowers and a little painting of the sea Lady Guilia had done that she had admired, and a wedding ring she and Jalal between them could never have afforded. And there was a magistrate, a kindly-seeming man who tried not to stare at Jalal, shocked because the Emperator's daughter—even a bastard daughter—was marrying a Domidian.

To her surprise, her father seemed pleased. He even shook Jalal's hand, wishing them well, and took both Serafina's hands in his, kissing her forehead, and she sensed she had made him happy. She wasn't sure why. It must be just his sense of propriety, she assumed, though it was said he had been more than wild in his youth. Well, there was no one so pious as a reformed reprobate.

And so they were married in front of the fireplace where Lady Guilia had served her tea. The words were read, she felt Jalal squeeze her hand reassuringly, and people signed any number of papers. She signed, too, wondering why she felt like she was signing her life away. Then she felt the baby kicking vigorously and remembered why. It wasn't only her life. Her child would be an Omani citizen. The benefits of that citizenship in their southern world were nearly incalculable.

She was Jalal's wife in truth. She didn't have to lie about that any more. Imrun had gotten his way, after all.

* * *

"THANK YOU," she told him, lying in bed with him that night. There would be no celebration in the bed chamber. She was about to give birth at any moment.

"For what?"

She smiled, looking over at him with her head on the pillow. He had trimmed his hair and beard for their ceremony, dressed far better than he usually did and behaved courteously, if quietly. He was always quiet, still not belonging anywhere. But he did belong to her, now. They would have to make their own little family. They really did not have another one.

"For coming," she said. "For being nice to everyone. I know you do not like them."

"I don't have to like them," he replied. "They are your people, not mine."

"Not really," she said. "Lissa likes me, but the rest? I don't think so. Lady Guilia is kind by nature, my father feels obligated, and my brother hates me. I believe he thinks I covet something."

"Don't you?" He gestured to their surroundings. "There is a lot here."

"Not for me," she said. "It has nothing to do with me, it never did."

"I'm glad you realize it."

"I do." She turned with an effort, facing him, taking his hand and placing it on her distended belly. "This is all we own."

He caressed her gently, his expression tender. "Actually, that is not true."

"What are you talking about?"

"Did you not read what you were signing?" he asked.

"Not, not really." She had been too nervous, just wanting it to be over.

"Your father has gifted us with land. Six hundred acres near the mountains in the north. Pasture land. It is the best place for horses. The water coming from those mountains makes strong bones and the air gives them good lungs."

She was too shocked to answer.

"He gave us horses, too," he added in a tone of deep irony. "Twenty-five. They are mine to train. He suggests I train cavalry mounts. They bring a good price."

Her mind was working again. "You mean..."

Jalal nodded, his eyes filled with mirth. "He has sold you for twenty-five horses. Just like any good Domidian father, except in this case he gave the horses, since I have nothing. I will sell them back to him, of course."

"Oh, the gods!" She began to gasp with helpless laughter, so intense that in a moment, tears were running from her eyes. Beside her, Jalal was trying to restrain himself.

"God above," she finally got out, "I begin to understand why that man is Emperator."

"I am sure it is not the only secret negotiation he has conducted," Jalal said, and they began laughing again.

"With Lady Guilia aiding him," Serafina accepted.

Jalal shrugged. "It's how the nobles work. She may actually like you. Still, she will do as she is told."

"So, they are kicking us out?"

"Not yet," Jalal told her. "The land comes after the baby is born. And then, of course, we have to build a house."

"Pitch a tent," she said. "I don't care. We have lived on the land before."

"Don't be bitter, now," Jalal admonished. "He has done very well by you, as far as he is concerned."

"I wanted to love him," she said softly.

Jalal just shook his head. "He doesn't want it."

"I thought he had some feeling for me," she lamented.

"He does. The feeling of relief that we will be gone."

She felt like she had been gutted, somehow—all her emotions drained. "I wanted to love him," she repeated, hollowly. All the hard travel and deprivation, all Jalal's doubts, none of that had broken her dream. But her father had. It was a magnificent bribe, but again, he wanted to be rid of her.

Jalal hitched himself up on one elbow, looking at her intensely. "I want it. Love me."

She reached up, touching the side of his face. This was the one she would know after all the others were gone. He had saved her life, probably more than once. She had fought for his and now they had made another one, between them. If that was not love, she didn't know what was.

"I do," she said.

She began to hiccup, unbalanced by her own laughter, now tinged with tears. Her father was as much a man of honor as Imrun. The real man was lying beside her. Carefully, he gathered her up, rocking her slowly until her hysterics were done.

"Shhh," Jalal soothed her, hand on her belly. Disturbed by her disturbance, the baby was kicking, as if in sympathy with her. "What do you think it is?"

"A boy," Serafina said.

She smiled, laying her hand over his.

"It is a boy," she repeated. "I will name this one Sahra—Al-Sahra, son of Jalal."

"You would name him for the desert?" Jalal questioned.

Serafina smiled again.

"He will live in the mountains. But he will be desert."

CHAPTER 20

The land looked like folds of green silk lifting and rippling in the wind.

"Look at that," Serafina said, awed. "It is like one of Lady Guilia's paintings." Her horse pawed impatiently as she checked him at the top of a high ridge from which they viewed their new home. All that green was grass, only waiting for him to eat it.

"Better," her husband replied. "It's real."

The day was fair, all blue sky and emerald grass and golden sun, and Serafina had to lift a hand to shade her eyes. Framed against faintly purplish foothills beyond the green swathe, figures of riders were barely discernible, specks of white in an orderly column. As she and Jalal watched, the line began a slow descent, coming in their direction like a caterpillar inching its way.

"They are exactly on time," he said. "Your father's arm has a long reach."

Serafina just smiled, looking down at the baby strapped to her. Cradled in a wool wrap holding him close, with the folds of her cloak falling around him, he was sharing her body heat. He had so much dark hair that the wind ruffled it and she put a gloved hand on his skull, shielding him. It made her next words sound oddly like a benediction.

"Welcome, Al-Sahra," she said, softly. "Welcome to your new home."

His dark eyes seemed to search her face. He did it frequently, bonding with her, but this time held special meaning for her.

"Yes," she said. "We are here."

Home was only a sea of waving grass at that moment—untouched by the hands of men. Behind them, two packhorses carried their few possessions. Those riding to meet them would bring the other things needed. Peering at them, Serafina realized some were women. Dressed almost exactly like the men in pantaloons and loose tunics, they were nearly indistinguishable from them except that they wore bright, trailing scarves fluttering in the wind like a garden of butterflies advancing across the shallow valley below.

She smiled. Here, she would be rid of the customs of Omani cities, where women went proudly bareheaded, announcing their freedom. She was free enough. Her fidelity to her husband was absolute. She was an honorable young wife and mother and if she chose the modesty of the scarf, it would not be because he doubted her.

The riders were drawing close enough to make out individual figures. They were young, most of them, with a few elders whose advice would be invaluable, while the younger ones provided labor. Their horses, fanning out, came at a carefully controlled canter up the slope, snorting in excitement at the sight of strange horses.

"Welcome!" one called. He was perhaps in his third decade and Serafina stared at him unashamedly, because she had rarely seen anyone with blond hair. He looked like sunlight, bold and dazzling, never moving in the saddle, like some kind of mythical creature.

"Hola," Jalal responded, using the universal greeting and glancing at her. "These are northern Omanis. They will not look like the others."

"So I see," she breathed. Most of them were blond or redheaded like her friend Patria, but all of them rode like desert warriors. What a strange assortment of people her father's country boasted. Yet her fate depended on them and she smiled in welcome. His money might pay them, but for people living nearly wild like this, money was not everything. If they liked her little family, it would go well. If not, it would not.

For her part, she already liked them.

"I am Javrik," the blond introduced himself, speaking Omani though he did not have an Omani name. Who were these people, anyway? "Where are your horses?"

"They will be coming," Jalal replied, "but not for some time. They need a place to live, too."

Javrik laughed. "We can make that." He nodded politely to Serafina, obviously not finding it odd that she had not been introduced. It was not expected. One did not flaunt their wives to strange men.

Turning in his saddle, he pointed down the rise to a spot where a creek wound like ribbon at the bottom.

"There would be your best spot, I think. Water, but not too much. Pasture. You have flat ground near the creek to work your horses, and not enough slope for an avalanche to come down on you in winter. That way..." he pointed behind them, in the direction they had come on barely-marked trails or none, "...you can drive them to sale, or sometimes buyers come here. There are Omani outposts. Sometimes they send buyers."

"Do they trouble you otherwise?" Jalal asked, because

those would be military posts.

The other man shook his head. "Rarely. We are peaceful, we pay our tax, they do not conscript our men and they buy our horses. It works well."

"You are Araks, mostly, are you not?"

Javrik nodded. "And some Omanis." He gave Jalal an assessing but not hostile glance. "You are a long way from home, friend."

"There are few horses in Domidia any more unless they are pulling carts," Jalal replied.

No, there was no disguising what her slim, dark husband was and no point in doing so. People here would either take to him or not.

The two men grinned at each other, a tie established. They were not men who would be driving any carts. Javrik already knew his descent from mountain men who had taken to the plains for better grazing, while Jalal's Domidian ancestors had raised the world's finest horses until Omana conquered them and took their assets. They spoke the same language—horse.

Turning again in his saddle as easily as if he had been sitting in his living quarters, Javrik beckoned to a young woman with long blond hair flowing beneath her scarf. "Sarai, come up."

Immediately, the woman who was probably his wife rode up, with a look of inquiry on her face.

"My wife, Serafina," Jalal said at once. Things were going in the proper order.

The other woman smiled at her, looking at Sahra.

"You have a baby!" she said delightedly. "We didn't know. How old?"

"He is four months," Serafina replied. She had ridden over three hundred miles miles from Xanthus only four months after giving birth.

The other riders were coming, circling them, the men beginning to talk with Jalal while the women were drawn to Sahra. Their cheerful voices formed a cacophony of welcome.

"I do not think I have ever seen a more beautiful baby," one of them said, earning Serafina's gratitude immediately.

"Thank you," she replied, clearing back some of his wrap so the admiring women could see his full head of dark hair and the faintly almond shaped dark eyes he had from Jalal. He was still fair skinned, like her, though. Really, he looked like both of them, which she liked. It seemed proper.

"Well, he will need shelter," one of the older women said, practically. "Usually, here we first put up a round shelter. Do you know those?"

Serafina just shook her head.

"They are good," the older one assured her. "I do not think you can have a house up before winter comes. We know those who come from outside like stone and timber, but ours do just as well and later they make a good playroom for children. We will build you one to stay in for now while the men start what you need for the animals."

She smiled at Serafina. "Their housing must come first or you will have nothing to eat."

It sounded like the women built the shelters. Was that possible? But looking at their casual seats astride on their horses, their sun-lined faces and competent air, somehow she could believe it. These were herders. What was it Jalal had called them—Araks?

Every Empire had people like these—those who had been there originally and were gobbled up by the ambitions of men like her father. If they remained peaceful, they could be left alone. Otherwise, they were annihilated.

This place was both her refuge and her exile and would be the home of her son, who would never know anything else. And perhaps, despite her dreams about Xanthus, that was for the best. Here, life would be a straightforward matter of survival, without the political pitfalls and perils of the capitol city.

"Thank you," she said. "I would be very grateful for the help."

"I am Ollind," the speaker introduced herself. "I have built many of these in my day. The supply train will come later. In the meantime, I suggest we have a fire and some tea. You have come a long distance."

Serafina glanced at Jalal, who just nodded, pulling his horse's rein to ride off with the men. It was wise to accept what people offered and far better for the baby. Though they had brought him in fair weather and been careful, he was still very young. A lean-to such as they had used during their travel was no place for an infant any longer than absolutely necessary.

"Good," she said.

Ollind turned, calling to the women, some of whom carried firewood strapped to their backs. Dismounting and unloading it, they joined the others who were kicking turf away from a promising spot and spread wood in a circular pattern, like a spider web. The men had already set up a tie line for horses, two stout posts with a sturdy line stretching between them, and were investigating another spot. While they cleared it of rocks and detritus, the industrious women set up a tripod and caldron, beginning to fill it with water from the stream and ladling in a good-smelling concoction they had carried with them in tins.

"Here is a spot for you," Sarai called, beckoning to Serafina to a place close to the fire. "We will sit with you for you to nurse the baby, if you like. He must be hungry by now."

He was. Serafina had begun hearing him whimper some time back and soon it would turn to full-blown, nerve-wracking demon-wailing, so she eased down from her horse with assistance from two of the women.

"He is precious cargo," one said with a smile. "Here, sit."

Shyly, she sat where her helper indicated, touched when another woman spread a woven blanket over her shoulders so that it sheltered both her and the baby. Though it was spring and she and Sahra were warmly dressed, still there was something in the air that was not yet entirely tamed. Immediately, those who were not working established themselves in a ring around her that both concealed her and blocked the wind. It blew ceaselessly on the open land, promising a kiss in summer and a blow in winter, with spring and fall somewhere between. Their cheery chatter was uplifting and, to her relief, all spoke Omani, so she could understand them. She heaved a sigh.

Ollind smiled at her understandingly, while the women with very young children held them and others supervised theirs at a distance. It was a convocation of mothers, sitting huddled under endless blue skies with children wild as deer, drinking tea and combing out each other's windswept hair, welcoming another one to their company.

Such were tribes, Serafina thought. She had never truly been in one, but she knew her ancestors had lived this way. When her father had exiled her to the furthest reaches of his empire, where she could be safely discounted, in reality he was returning her to the life her mother's people had lived in Domidia.

Al-Sahra, son of Jalal, would live that way. She smiled down at him as he nursed, now content. In the distance, his father was pacing with the other men, establishing a site for their round tent. Horses stood hipshot under their loads while dogs and children ran on the outskirts of what was becoming a camp, barking and laughing. She drew a deep breath, relishing the clean air. It was the air of freedom.

CHAPTER 21

By afternoon, the supply train had come, mud sledges pulled by horses, sliding over the still-firm earth more easily than they might have done if it had, in fact, been muddy.

"These work now," Ollind told her, "but they are best in snow. That is a long way off, though. We have done what we can."

That appeared to have been quite a bit. The sledges were piled high with cargo that had mainly been rolled and strapped in hides. Serafina could not do much while holding Sahra, so she watched as stalwart women unloaded the sledges except for the heaviest things. One item did require the men to remove it—a heavy cast iron stove recognizable as the same type she and Jalal had used in their cheap apartment in Xanthus. This one looked new. This would be an extremely precious item in the north, imported from elsewhere at great trouble and expense. Most likely it had been purchased at an Omani outpost. They were the only ones who could get such things, brought in by Army pack trains.

"That will be your heat and your cook fire," Ollind

explained, as if apprehensive that she had never used one before.

But Serafina was not that backwards. "Yes, I know that kind."

"Good." Ollind called to the other women from time to time, but it hardly seemed necessary. First, they laid boards neatly notched together to make a centerpiece, than unrolled mats of close-tied branches on all four sides of it. Once again, the men were pressed into service to unload three long poles joined at the top, placing them carefully at the circumference of what would be the shelter, evenly spaced. With that accomplished, they returned to marking out livestock pens, leaving the women to painstakingly unload and erect other long poles, evenly spaced, all resting in the croft of the three main uprights.

It took a long time, usually requiring two women to raise each. After a while, Sarai left the others to come and sit with her, drinking more tea.

"You may learn this," she said, sipping, "but for now just watch. You have your baby and no knowledge of how to do it."

It was a simple statement of fact, said in a tone of voice that conveyed it as such.

"You have done this often?" Serafina inquired.

"Oh, time out of mind," Javrik's wife assured her. "This is how we lived, for the most part, until the Omanis came and made a border at the river. Many of us still do."

"They do not trouble you?" Serafina asked, just as Jalal had.

"Hardly ever," Sarai asserted. "The Domidians, now, they were trouble. Our men fought them at the mountain passes. Other tribes from the north crossed over to help us, which they rarely do, but the Domidians would never have stopped at the border. They would have slaughtered everyone. Fortunately, they cannot fight in snow. We pushed them back. Then someone else drove them out and the Omanis came. They gave us gifts for what they called our help, though we were not trying to help them, and treated us fairly, and everyone went home."

"Havacians," Serafina said softly. "They did it, and others from the north."

"We did not see those," Sarai said.

"Well, you're lucky. They know how to fight in snow and they are savages."

"Ah." It was Sarai's only comment.

"My husband is peaceable," she tried to reassure the other woman. "He will not cause you problems."

Sarai just shrugged. "All are welcome if they can live here. Not everyone can. The land defeats many of them and they die or leave."

Had her father given them land there because he did not expect them to survive? She supposed it was possible. On the other hand, people agreed it was the finest place in Omana to raise horses and Jalal's heart was set on that.

"Well, I have never seen snow," she laughed, not wanting to think about it. "We will see if I can."

Javrik's wife turned to look at her closely.

"You two rode from Xanthus alone, and with a small baby? Yes, I think you will make it here. You have good backing, too, it seems. The Omanis have paid us very well for our help."

Serafina just nodded.

"We are grateful for the money, mind you. But your husband may at some point want to go the border and see if he can pick up others crossing over for work. You are going to need workers here. We have few to spare."

They might be few, but they knew what to do. The ribs of the shelter were nearly complete, leaving a gap for a door, and the women were unloading simple furniture—tables, mostly—and spacing them inside the circle, then throwing down thick rugs over the woven mats. Woven in every color, they were rich as jewels.

"Javrik!" Sarai called, and her husband raised his head alertly. "The stove."

He nodded, calling to several of the men. It would take all of them to carry the heavy stove inside, placing it on a platform of bricks the women had laid as a base, attaching a stove pipe and pushing it up to where the poles formed an opening at the top. As the women stood back, panting from their efforts, men pushed it into place with a great deal of grunting and cursing, most of it good natured.

"Excellent," Sarai said, gesturing to where sturdy poles were being pushed sideways through the ribs, being secured to an upright so that they hung over the stove. "There will be your tripod to cook on, do you see? We will hang chains for your pots."

Serafina nodded, impressed.

"In the hills are many trees for fuel," Sarai told her. "The stove will burn anything—wood or dung or coal from places we have found. We will show you. We will leave you a sledge to bring in a supply. You can use your pack horses."

"It's going to be a great deal of work living here," Serafina observed.

"Yes." Sarai smiled, touching Sahra's head lightly as he drifted off to sleep. "Have many children. You will need them all. We will help you when you have another."

"Where do the rest of you live?"

"Over the foothills. Half a day's ride." She looked at Serafina quizzically. "This is Omani land and they do not part with it. How did you come by this?"

"It was a wedding present," Serafina said.

Sarai raised her brows. "You must have wealthy friends."

Serafina smiled. "Just one."

"We have gotten payment from their outpost," Sarai told her. "We are glad to help, but we must work quickly so that you have enough to survive the winter."

Serafina looked thoughtfully at the sloping meadows and foothills around them—so beautiful, so peaceful, so deceptive. Covered with snow, they would not be so friendly. They would be lucky to make it.

But that was what people had said about their trek from Domidia, too—that they had been lucky to survive.

Fascinated, she watched as the women unrolled the hides she had seen rolled on the sledges. They were massive.

"This is the fun part," Sarai said. It didn't look like much fun. Using long poles, the women began painstakingly sliding heavy hides up the sides of the shelter and stretching them. Sinew threaded through the tops hooked over the upright poles, then more hard-working women repeated the maneuver with yet more hides, fur turned to the inside, then repeated the whole thing with another whole layer of hides, fur side out.

"I get dizzy just watching them," Serafina commented.

Sarai shrugged. "If it was too much for us, we would call the men. But they are busy and anyway, now comes the decoration. Here, you can help."

"Really?" Serafina didn't see how, but she rose, slinging Sahra carefully in his carry blanket, grateful that he was worn out and sleeping. He had nursed, had his cloth changed, and was warm and secure. It took little to make him happy, though he would awaken like a little tiger.

"Come," Sarai repeated, leading her through the opening that still remained. A hole had been cut in the hide above it, admitting some sunlight, but otherwise the entire shelter was dim and cozy. Serafina recognized hooks for oil lamps, though. They could make it brighter.

And now women were carrying in bundles of what looked like rags, but beautiful rags in every different color and pattern, all of them heavily quilted. Standing or kneeling, they were beginning to thread them through the framework of poles, weaving them just like looming a rug. It made a fairy palace out of a tent of hides—beautiful and colorful.

"Here," Sarai said, handing her a bundle. "Fix it how you like it."

It was fun, decorating with the chattering women making her a home, and Serafina worked with a will, keeping her arms carefully above the sleeping baby. He appeared lulled by the rhythm of her body and the warmth in the tent. Even without the stove, it was warm.

"You have bedrolls with you?" Sarai inquired, and Serafina nodded. "Bring them in, you can tuck them beneath the bottom layer of rags. You will be perfectly warm. Hang whatever you like—lamps, beads, anything pretty. It is yours now. You can use this when it is cool, and your lean-to shelter when it is hot. You will catch a good breeze here and there is water. Make your private place downstream, where the water will carry away whatever you put in it."

That would be the latrine, apparently. But if she had ever doubted it, that established that she was on the frontier now. Jalal could probably build something better, later.

Carefully, she picked her way back out through the space where women were making a hide-covered flap for a door and back to her own packhorses, now tethered. Only one item traveled packed with extreme care, but it was the only one she wanted.

Returning inside, she unwrapped the silk-covered packet that contained her other wedding present from Lady Guilia.

"What is that?" Sarai asked at once in a tone of wonder, and the other women gathered around, exclaiming over the painting.

"Is that the ocean?" one asked, and Serafina nodded. They were landlocked here, unable to see any ocean, so the painting fascinated them.

"A friend did this for our wedding," she half explained. There was no need to explain that it was her father's wife, the Royal Consort, who painted. It was a new world, a new life. She must leave all that behind her.

Xanthus was gone for her. It had been a child's dream, and now she thought she might regret it for the rest of her life. It had resulted in great material possessions, granted, but her father had plenty of those. It took merely a dip into his treasury to be rid of her. What she really valued—his love, his acknowledgement—she would never get. She had left her mother to find her father and now had neither of them. He had been kind, he had been generous, but his air of detachment had been unmistakable. He had a family and she was not part of it. She was an unexpected complication, while the baby she bore he viewed as merely a youthful mistake. One might have thought he would pay more attention to his first grandchild, but he had barely looked at Sahra except to say he seemed healthy.

"Oh, that is so beautiful," Sarai admired Lady Guilia's work. "Where will you put it?"

"Maybe above one of the tables? Will the shelter take on rain?" Serafina asked.

"No." Sarai shook her head firmly. "Every inch of hides is waterproofed and we do them again every year when we take down the shelters. Yours is freshly done. It will be good all year. We get little rain, anyway—it is mainly snow here, and that only helps to insulate the walls."

She watched critically as Serafina hung her painting with care. That, at last, wakened Sahra.

"He wants to play," Sarai observed, "Look how he

stretches his arms and legs. Oh, he is a strong one. Put him on your bedroll. We will watch him."

Ollind came up behind them, putting a hand lightly on Serafina's arm. "We will. You have hardly had him out of your arms for hours and we would adore playing with him. Why do you not take a break outside?" She glanced at the bottom of the shelter, where hands showed beneath the tent from outside, busy strapping down the poles now that everything was in place. "We are finished here."

Serafina emerged in a fog. She had been so preoccupied with the human shelter that she had not watched the men at work. Now she could see that a long low shed for livestock was up, with fencing of simple interlocked branches laced to uprights. It would hold small creatures like sheep and goats. Horses would require much more.

The fire circle was being used again. From somewhere, someone had obtained the butchered carcass of a sheep already spitted and hung without her notice. It would take a long time to roast. In the meantime, smaller rabbits and birds hung skewered and beginning to drip fat. There would be food and she was ready. Tea would only do just so much. Their guests had arranged their own shelters and hobbled a few mares wearing bells around their necks. The others grazed and took water freely, but they would not go far from the lead mares, following the sound of their bells in the dark, and those could not go far. The dogs and a few men with small fires would guard them all night and they would come for grain in the morning.

Seeing her emerge, Jalal walked away from the other men, coming to her.

"We have a shelter," she said, stretching up to hold his shoulders even though she knew others were watching. This was her man; she could hold him if she liked, and she liked, resting her head against his chest. He smelled of wood smoke and curved his arms around her. She did not mind if others saw them. Several months in Xanthus had taught her a great deal about the power and persistence of rumors. It was too much to hope that word would not eventually leak out that the Emperator had given this land. Then, she might well be viewed as his cast-off mistress. Let people see something else.

"The baby?" he asked.

"Inside with the women. They adore him."

"Of course they do." He massaged her back gently through her cloak. "You can use a break. Come and sit by the fire."

Others were beginning to gather there and she made her way through them, holding his hand, smiling shyly at people she did not yet know. She was still dressed Omani-style and the people were perfectly friendly, but she turned at a gentle touch on her shoulder.

It was a young girl she did not recognize, holding out a length of green and purple and white cloth, very recognizably a headscarf. There were men present now, making it proper to cover her hair. Smiling her thanks, Serafina wrapped it expertly around the crown of her head, knotting it, with the tails trailing down in a beautiful streamer on one side. She did not even have to look. Her hands remembered.

Looking up, she saw Jalal's satisfied expression. He would not wear his turban again; that was too Domidian. But he was pleased that she had so quickly adopted the garb of these people. With one act, she had announced her willingness to be one of them...her possible kinship with at least some of the traditions they observed.

"You are beautiful," he said. "Come and eat."

CHAPTER 22

"Are those wolves?" Serafina asked as darkness fell.

In the hills behind them, the weird ululating cries of animals she had never heard until then raised the hair on her arms. They did not have them in Domidia and Xanthus had been the city, far removed from nature.

Javrik laughed softly, not unkindly.

"They will not hurt you. They are only calling to each other, gathering their pack. There are plenty of deer for them to eat."

But he looked over at Jalal. "We will put doors on your shed in the morning and leave you a couple of cur dogs when we go. Once they know the boundaries of your land, they will defend them from anything trying to cross over. They cannot take down a wolf, of course, but it will give you warning. Keep a good supply of arrows, and torches. We will show you where to find pitch. They are afraid of fire."

Serafina shivered.

"Put donkeys in with your horses as we do," he advised. "They hate wolves. Horses will run, but donkeys will fight."

"Can we get up at least a small barn for the horses we have with us?" Jalal asked.

"Yes, and a loft," Javrik replied. "So you can make hay this summer." He was stretched at his leisure, munching on one of the game birds the women had spitted and roasted, basted with honey. Serafina thought she had seldom tasted anything so good in her life. The sheep was still roasting, promising mutton later in the night or even in the morning, when it would be equally welcome. Warm and fed, with friendly company and the baby propped against her, playing with smooth stones, she felt a contentment that had eluded her everywhere else.

Here, there seemed to be no sentiment against them because they were Domidian, and she wondered if it was because life was just so difficult that people must get along or die. It had been the same in the caravan. This reminded her of it.

"We can stay long enough to help you," Javrik said, "and my friend Dom will be here by morning with a small flock and some of the donkeys I mentioned. That will get you started. You will need wool to live here."

"Dom?" Serafina questioned. That, at last, was an Omani name she recognized.

Javrik smiled at her. "We marry with Omanis, sometimes. Even the Emperator's line has some Arak in it."

That got her attention. "It does?"

"Yes." He discarded a few bones, immediately snatched up by dogs. "It goes far back. His grandfather's mother was a Linardo. They are intermarried with Araks. They and the Viespis were powerful northern families, with vast estates. Then they married with Magistris. All of them are dead now, I think."

"Maybe not all." Serafina spoke softly, thoughtfully,

instinctively glancing at Sahra. "What else do you know of them?"

The tribal leader shrugged. "Only what everyone does."

Everyone but me, Serafina thought resentfully. Family history had not been shared with her, because she was not family.

"We did not expect another Emperator," Javrik said, "especially not one from Havacia. But his foreign Omani descent does go back to the great general, Magistri, so they chose him because everyone else was dead."

"Doesn't seem like much of a reason," Jalal commented.

"Better than none, I would suppose." Javrik helped himself to another game bird, swearing softly as it burned his fingers. Serafina just smiled. It was spitted, but he had neglected to take the ends of the spit, which would not have burned. Men were too brave for their own good, sometimes.

"He doesn't bother us," Javrik noted. "For taxes, yes, but nothing else. We can live with him."

"The Empiratis couldn't," Jalal noted.

"Only some of them." Javrik was no longer singeing his fingers. "And that was because he outlawed the slave trade. They had been making fortunes from it. Of course they tried to kill him."

"And failed."

Javrik nodded.

"He had been friendly with the people before then. After that, he was not as much. His cousin is King of Havacia, with a vast army he could call in if he wanted, so the people subsided. He was so set on abolishing slavery that there was no moving him from it. But I do not think anyone trusted anyone after that."

It confirmed what Serafina had felt. In many ways, her father was a cold and lonely man despite the charm he could wield when he wished—not the one her mother had described, nor Lady Guilia, either. Life must have changed him.

"They will be happier with his son, I think," Javrik said.

Serafina barely avoided choking, exchanging an ironic look with Jalal.

But her husband said nothing.

"Prince Dario is more Omani," Javrik judged. "After all, the Emperator is half Havacian from his mother and mixed with Alcinis from his father. He does as well by us as he can, but the people seem to think Dario will be better."

That was a matter of opinion, Serafina thought, but she followed Jalal's lead, remaining silent except for one thing.

"The Emperator is Alcini, as well?" she questioned. Jalal had said they were all crazy.

"Assuredly. His grandmother was Queen Tia, the great Queen in the north. She was taken captive when Tumagis raided Alcinia to get tin for the Emperator, Iberis, and ended up here as a slave. It is said that is why Emperator Sergius was so determined to free the slaves."

"What happened to her?" Serafina asked, fascinated. Men were taught these things, she supposed. Women were not, at least not in Domidia.

"General Magistri married her," Javrik said, "and then took the throne in Alcinia through her while Domidians conquered Omana. He never returned. She had children with him and then, after his men killed him, married the prince who became King of Havacia. Her son by the General is the Emperator's father, his daughter is Queen in Alcinia and the other one heads the Holy Sisters, the sorceresses of the north. The King of Havacia now is her grandson from the second husband and his uncle led the Navy that invaded Domidia."

He tossed away another bone, laughing. "You could say her children conquered the world."

"You are well informed for someone living as a nomad," Jalal observed.

Javrik cast his spit back into the fire, letting it burn, apparently finished with his meal. "This is my land. I learn what I need to know to hold it."

He did not look so harmless now, Serafina thought. She supposed if those herders had retreated to the narrow mountain passes, they might well have been able to defend them, especially assisted by their kin. They might only be a thorn in the side of an Emperator, but a painful one. Obviously, he had deemed it better to keep them as allies, gifting them and exempting their men from military service. Those were huge concessions from any ruler. Of course, it also kept potential rebels from being trained by his commanders, learning his army.

"I thought you got along with the Omanis," she ventured.

Javrik's blue eyes gleamed in semi-darkness. "I do today."

People were drifting from the campfire, one by one, putting their children to bed. There were more days of hard work ahead of them. And then, Serafina thought with a wrench, they would depart. She had been enjoying their company.

"You should go to the border for workers," Javrik commented to Jalal, closing the other subject. "Bring them back before we go so that Serafina is not left here alone. It is not safe for her."

"You do not mind more Domidians?" Jalal questioned.

"Not if they are like you. We need settlers so long as they are peaceful ones."

"Many of our people were peaceful," Jalal said softly, and Serafina knew he was remembering things that had happened to him. "It did not save us from the ambitions of our rulers."

Javrik stood up abruptly. “It never does. They will always buy our horses, because of it. I will see you in the morning.”

He strode outside the light of the fire circle, pausing only to greet his wife, putting an arm around her as they walked back towards one of the small hide shelters the Araks had erected. Serafina could see Sarai’s strong face in profile as she turned her head, looking up at her husband and reaching to stroke his beard while his hand cradled her backside.

She and Jalal smiled at each other. “We should go,” he said, reaching for Sahra, who was beginning to nod with his head against her.

“Yes, we have a home now,” she agreed, with a frisson of pleasure. They did have a home, a place where they might resume their marriage. It had been too difficult, traveling and living in a lean-to with a frequently screaming baby. “Come and see it.”

Jalal lit one of the oil lamps as they went in. The flickering light roused the baby, who began to whine.

“He needs his cloth changed,” Serafina said, smiling and caressing the back of one of his little legs as he twisted in his father’s arms. “I will do it.”

What she had first seen as Jalal’s indifference to her pregnancy had simply been a matter of his usual silence. There was no question now that he was deeply attached to his son, even to the point of being willing to change his cloths, to hold him, play with him and tell him stories he was too young to understand, but would not always be. He was proud of his son’s Domidian name and that she had chosen it.

Now Sahra turned and Serafina took him, happy to have a table where she had put his cloths and could lay him on top to do what was necessary. He was not helpful, kicking and squirming, so Jalal stood at the head, tickling his cheeks and distracting him until the baby was smiling and gurgling.

“Here we go,” Serafina said, finishing and hoisting him,

unlacing her bodice. To her relief, he was a good sleeper and a brief period of nursing should be followed by at least a few hours of peace. Quietly, she paced the limited confines of their shelter with him until he was satisfied, then sat him on one of the bedrolls she had put, as suggested, next to a quilted wall too snuggly secured for him to roll under it.

"He will be safe here," she told Jalal, tucking him carefully into place, then letting him hold her fingers with one chubby fist, stroking his soft hair gently as he tumbled into sleep. "This is how the other women sleep their children."

"Good." He pulled back their bedroll, right next to the baby's. "Why don't you take your clothes off and come to bed?"

It was pleasantly warm in the shelter, the oil light flickered just enough for them to see each other and she sighed happily, watching him watch her. She knew that intent expression. This would be a good night.

"It's been too long," she said, sinking into their bedroll. Shedding his clothes like a snake shed its skin, Jalal crawled in immediately, before the baby could wake, and Serafina giggled, thinking that they were like bad children trying to evade their parents.

"Ahh," she sighed in bliss, hugging him full length, offering herself unashamedly.

"Greedy," he admonished softly, smiling at her.

"How else will I have another baby?" she teased, running both hands down his sides, treasuring the feel of his body on hers. He was not large by comparison with the big Arak men, but she knew his strength and took a visceral, animal pleasure in the sensation of submitting to him. It was more than that, now—no longer solely an act of passion, but one of lust intermingled with so much tenderness it was hard to know where one ended and the other began.

"Do you want one?" He sounded surprised.

"Do you realize our children will be the descendants of great people?" she countered. "An Emperator, a Queen, people who conquered the world."

"Only by an accident of birth," he reminded her, leaning over her, stroking back her hair. "We have nothing in common with those people."

"Don't we?"

"No," he murmured, lips on her body, learning her all over again. She shivered in pleasure, wondering if all women enjoyed this as much as she did. She had heard women complain of their husbands, but she had no such qualms about Jalal. To feel his life force inside her and his heart beating against hers gave her something so profound, it was indescribable, and the longer she was with him, the greater it grew.

"I will make a home for you here, a real home," he said, kissing the line of her collarbone and down her shoulder as she curved her hand over his neck. "Someday, if you like, perhaps your mother would wish to come."

Working his way up again, he ran his tongue along the tendons of her neck, teasing with gentle bites. "Let her leave Imrun with his little treasures."

Her heart leapt in hope. "Do you really think so?"

He had reached her face, hands cradling her head as he kissed her forehead, her eyes, finally her mouth.

"Yes," he murmured.

Moving against him, she asked without words for his love. It had been hers for the taking, all along.

She was descended from a woman whose sons had conquered the world.

Now, let them see what the desert bred.

THE END

ABOUT THE AUTHOR

Fantasy poetry driven by myths and legends has been my passion for as long as I can remember. I was published in poetry before catching the romance writing bug. I bring that background to my writing along with a lifelong addiction to horses, an 18 year career in various areas of psychiatric social services and many trips to Ireland, where I nurture my muse. My published works range from contemporary fantasy romance to fantasy historical, futuristic, science fiction and historical romance. Currently I live in rural Pennsylvania with a "motley crew" of rescue animals.

Find my other books: https://miriamnewman.com/

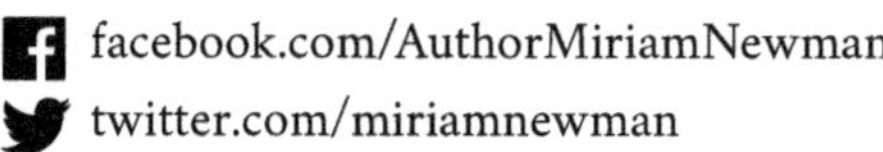

www.ingramcontent.com/pod-product-compliance
Lightning Source LLC
La Vergne TN
LVHW050541160826
845677LV00011B/2128

* 9 7 9 8 8 4 7 8 9 8 9 3 5 *